T0148290

Who Cares
Who Milks the Cow

Peggy Bergland

iUniverse, Inc.
Bloomington

Who Cares Who Milks the Cow

iUniverse books may be ordered through booksellers or by contacting:

iUniverse
1663 Liberty Drive
Bloomington, IN 47403
www.iuniverse.com
1-800-Authors (1-800-288-4677)

ISBN: 978-1-4759-3862-3 (sc)
ISBN: 978-1-4759-3863-0 (e)

Printed in the United States of America

iUniverse rev. date: 9/17/2012

Acknowledgements

The encouragement my neighbors, Hedy Logan and her daughter Suzy, gave to me while writing this story was what made me keep at writing. Many mornings we sat on her front porch with a cup of coffee and a pleasant conversation to start the day. Her cup of coffee was always welcome as I never seem to have conquered the ability to make a good cup of coffee, and hers was always good. Suzy would come over to my house to see that there were no weeds growing around the yard. I think she was afraid I would hurt myself trying to pull them out, since I am the ancient age of eighty-six. This did give me time to spend at my computer. They both urged me to keep on. My daughter, Judi, was also a great help. I could call on her to come over and straighten out my computer whenever it gave me fits and it got balky and refused to work the way I wanted it to. You see, I did not have anything to do with computers until I was at least eighty-three years of age when I decided I wanted to learn how to operate the darn contraption. Gee, when I went to high school they didn't even have electric typewriters so I was not fortunate enough to be around a new fangled gadget like a computer until my later years. Now I love it.

Chapter 1

The Wedding

THE STORY-BOOK ROMANCE Martha had with Jackson seemed to be the one any girl would dream of. She thought he was the man of her dreams. His handsome features attracted any girl who saw him. He was about six feet two with blond curly hair that most girls wished they had. He had a personality that would win almost anyone, man or woman and seemed to be very gracious to all he met. Jackson was very attentive to her and everyone seemed to like him. Her family was happy that such a wonderful man was to marry their Martha. Friends held several engagement parties for the couple.

They had a huge wedding which was attended by over one hundred friends and relatives. They came by train, horse-drawn wagons and carriages, and a few by automobile, although automobiles were not yet very popular as a means of transportation as they would become at a later time. The roads were not very conducive for much automobile travel. They were muddy and full of ruts and almost impassable whenever it rained. Anyway you could always depend on your faithful horses to get you there under all circumstances. Fortunately the weather turned out to be beautiful. The reception went well and friends helped put all the gifts into a wagon to be delivered to the home of the bride and groom at a later time. What a perfect day for such a lovely wedding of a beautiful couple.

Martha was not a ravishing beauty, but she was considered very attractive with brown eyes, dark blond hair that might even be considered light brown, and she was five feet three inches tall. She was nineteen years old when she married Jackson. She was a very friendly woman whose personality was most pleasant, and was well liked by all who knew her. She would do everything she could to help others, and go out of her way to do so. People could confide in her and she would keep their confidence. In a way, this was a short-coming she had that worked against her, and in the long run could be something that was harmful.

The newlyweds headed to the bride's farmhouse, which was in a beautiful setting among lovely old trees with a small creek not very far from the house. The house was about a quarter of a mile from the main road down a tree lined lane which Martha's grandfather had planted decades before. There were the usual outbuildings that went with a farm. This was a place which, with a little work, could be made very easily into a showplace they could be proud of. Martha had inherited it from her grandparents who had realized the potential for the property. All it would take would be a little work. It had a great potential. They would have a good start with a few head of cattle to start a herd, and two nice saddle horses as well as a team to do farm work. Martha could almost be considered wealthy with such a good financial start for this marriage.

They arrived after a short travel time. They did not expect any guests to come to the farmhouse as they had such a grand party at the reception. Upon arriving home is where his true personality really showed up.

"You go in and change out of your fancy dress while I put the horses away" is what she heard him tell her. She went into the house and headed for the bedroom and slowly removed her wedding dress, kicked off her shoes and was ready to put on her plain housedress when he came into the bedroom. She shyly faced him expecting a tender kiss and a few sweet words. Instead he screamed at her "I told you to undress, not just to change your clothes" and he grabbed her and ripped off her undergarments while throwing her onto the bed violently. Shocked and stunned at his sudden sign of violence toward her, she submitted out of sheer terror. Martha had thought he was the man of her dreams. She was surprised and greatly shocked when he turned violent towards her.

When Jackson finally let her up he informed her she was not to ever argue with him about anything he did or wanted. Also, he did not want her to have anything further to do with her own family or friends now that she was his property. His violence was so sudden and very unexpected, especially on their wedding day of all times, that she was too terrified to even think. He had been very clever in hiding his violence until this very moment.

Martha soon realized that she was also a prisoner of sorts and that no one else seemed to notice her predicament. He was clever at covering up why she no longer visited her friends or family. As newlyweds they needed some privacy is what her family and friends probably thought. If they only knew. Because of his threats that he would harm her family if she complained to them, she was afraid to approach anyone for help.

After they had been married only a few months, she discovered she was pregnant. When she told Jackson, instead of being happy about it, he became more abusive towards her and even hit her with the possible intention of having her lose the baby. For months Martha struggled through the sickness of the pregnancy, feeling sick most of the time with the premonition that all was not well with either herself or the baby.

The baby turned out to be a little girl, born a month premature, and she was not a healthy child. In fact, the doctor told Martha he doubted if the child would live to be even a year old. How devastating this was. In spite of Jackson's abuse, she had looked forward to this child. She even hoped his attitude would change, which was a hope that was not realized. The baby would frequently cry because of being sick and he had not patience or understanding with the child. In fact, Martha worked very hard to see that the baby was comfortable so she would not cry. Jackson's attitude was hard to understand, but fortunately he did not physically harm the baby. He just did not understand that a baby did not cry unless she was ill or very uncomfortable.

It was about the time baby Sarah was three months old that Jackson informed Martha that he was selling their farm, and that they were moving further West where they would not be bothered with people he did not want her to see. Martha was now more frightened than ever, but felt so helpless because of this isolation. She did not know what to do about it. Then, too, there was baby Sarah that she would have to look out for. Sarah was listless and needed lots of care and who would do it if she couldn't? Martha felt she had to put up with Jackson's abuse for the sake of her baby. At least he took out his nastiness on her and not on helpless Sarah.

Jackson sold off all the livestock, found a buyer for the farm. and made all arrangements to travel by train to Idaho or Oregon, telling Martha they were going to leave immediately. He wouldn't even tell her or her family where they were going. She would have to find out on her own. Had he schemed to marry her to gain her inheritance, which was worth quite a bit? What could she do? Jackson was showing all the signs that he was dangerous. She was at a complete loss except to do what he told her to. Since she was the one who had inherited the farm from her grandparents, how could he sell it. Maybe he would forge her signature or force her to sign to sell the property.

She had to think of baby Sarah first of all didn't she? Since Sarah was so weak Martha had to do everything possible to care for her and to protect her the best she could. The worry was always there because of the warning from the doctor that she might not last to be a year old. Under the circumstances she just could not take a chance and defy her abusive mate. She had to protect her baby no matter what happened.

An unexpected visit from her mother's brother, Uncle Curtis Verne Andrews, was a pleasant surprise to Martha.

She was quite happy to see him. It had been a long time since he had visited with the family. Curtis informed Martha he had been busy overseeing some business for her mother. About this time Uncle Curtis noticed that her eyes were red and swollen. It was very evident she had been crying. When he asked her what her troubles were, she tried to avoid telling him about her abusive husband, but could not stop herself from sobbing. She tried to cover it over by telling him about Sarah being weak and ill, and that the doctor had warned her that little Sarah might not live to be a year old. This was devastating news, of course. When she seemed reluctant to talk about her own troubles, Uncle Curtis decided to let it go for the time being and started to tell her about her mother's plans. He was helping her mother negotiate with a rancher from Mesa Ridge, Idaho interested in buying all her livestock. Martha and Curtis both realized that ever since Martha's father had suddenly died last year, it had been too much for her mother to run the farm without hired help. It was best that Jean dispose of her livestock and the man from Idaho was very interested in buying all of what was available. Her mother was also considering the possibility of selling the farm. Although Martha's mother, Jean, was still fairly young, at forty-five, the farm was more than a lone woman could handle. Maybe the nice gentleman from Idaho would help her to sell the farm. According to Uncle Curtis her mother was very impressed with the man, and so was he. They were both sure he was not only helpful but honest. They were encouraged by his attitude. He even invited both Jean and Curtis to visit him some day if they ever came to Mesa Ridge, Idaho. They said they would consider it, and even might make definite plans to visit in the future. Mesa Ridge sounded like an interesting place. Uncle Curtis even mentioned that he might come out there to look around at some property as he was wanting to find something he could develop. But that was only a dream at this time.

"*What will Mother do then*," wondered Martha. She had no more than thought those words when Jackson walked into the house. He was his usual surly self and without even a decent greeting or even asking who he was, demanded that Uncle Curtis should leave.

Martha spoke up and told Jackson, "This is my uncle and I do not want him to leave". Jackson then viciously turned on Martha and told her she had better shut up her mouth or he would shut it for her. When Curtis tried to say something Jackson took an unexpected swing at him and Curtis responded right back in a very also unexpected way. Jackson was not used to anyone opposing him. Of course with his usual bullying attitude, Jackson evidently thought he could intimidate this man as he had Martha. What a big mistake that was. To his surprise, Uncle Curtis was not taking this kind of abuse from Jackson or anyone else and he resented the abuse to Martha also. He immediately figured out what Martha had been going through and did not hesitate to respond to Jackson with a right to the jaw, following this with a kick behind his knees which made Jackson fall to the floor. Curtis stepped back and let him get up. Jackson then grabbed a chair and tried to use it as a weapon against Curtis. Curtis was not to be intimidated by such a move and grabbed the chair from Jackson and threw it back out of reach. Martha stood back, watching the fight, worrying that her uncle would end up killing Jackson, which would make for more troubles. Jackson was not using any sense and rushed at Curtis again but Curtis was expecting such a move and again side-stepped away from him. Uncle Curtis let go with a jab to the ribs and then to his belly. Jackson dove at Curtis, suddenly grabbing him around the legs and trying to trip him. Being an experienced fighter, Uncle Curtis was able to dodge Jackson's attempt to trip him. Jackson was losing his temper more and more which made it easier for Curtis to figure out what Jackson was trying to do. Evidently Jackson was no fighter with this kind of experience. He usually only used bullying words to intimidate people and had evidently gotten away with it in the past. Not this time. Curtis finally grabbed Jackson by his arms and twisted one behind his back, holding him there until he could be calmed down enough to listen to Curtis.

"I could beat you to a pulp, Jackson, but I won't because of my niece, but if I ever hear you talk like that to her again I will be back and finish this job. Do you hear me?" With a nod of his head, Jackson showed he understood and agreed. Uncle Curtis than left after informing Martha he would see her again later. "If Jackson takes this confrontation out on you, just let me know and I will finish the job."

Right after Curtis left, Jackson told Martha to finish packing because they were leaving in the morning. When Martha said she was going to let her family know where they were going he told her she was not going to let them know anything. With that he got trunks out for her to pack a few more of the things they were taking with them. Some of her possessions were packed into one of the trunks and then he insisted she use one medium size steamer trunk to pack baby clothes, especially the ones she was not yet using. She was told to take only a minimum of anything else that belonged to her. It would cost too much to ship stuff she did not need. It occurred to her that it was odd he was so very protective of the trunk with the baby clothes but not the other items. Maybe he had some kind of feelings after all toward the baby that he didn't have for anyone else except himself. Although it wasn't like Jackson to think of the baby any more than he did of anyone else, she dismissed the trunk from her thoughts until many months later.

Martha packed as much as she could in the largest trunk and used the one for the baby clothes to pack all the very nicest of the clothes that the baby would grow into at a later time. Most of these clothes were hand made gifts that had been given her by her friends and neighbors. They were treasures she was glad that Jackson seemed to want.

Chapter 2

They Board A Train

Even if she could have had a chance to inform her mother as to where they were going, it would have been hard under the circumstances. Martha knew her mother was struggling very hard since her father had passed away. Her mother, Jean, had had too much to do to keep up the farm and take care of the cattle. Jean's brother, Curtis, had been doing everything he could, but all the work had even been too much with his help. There was not enough money left any more to hire the amount of help that was needed. Things had seemed pretty bad for Jean, until the man from Mesa Ridge purchased the farm animals. It was beginning to look like everything was working out for her mother The man from Mesa Ridge seemed to be a very big help to both Jean and her uncle Curtis. This was a big relief to Martha's mind that her mother would be all right, especially since Jackson had gained control of everything

Martha owned and he was not inclined to help any of her family unless it was to his advantage. Martha had spent many a night crying herself to sleep. She even had to do that silently to avoid Jackson's abuse.

All their few meager belongings that had not been sold were loaded on a train. Jackson still did not inform Martha where they were going. He would not even give her a chance to see her family so she could not tell them where or when they were going. Jackson had only told Martha that they were going "West" and that she did not need to know anything more. Of course she was very frightened but did not know what else to do about it except to go along and hope that she could handle things at a later date. She also knew she would have to be brave for the sake of Sarah, but if anything happened to the baby, she would leave Jackson and go to her mother as bad as she would hate to have to go back and ask for her help. In the meantime it was best not to upset Jackson. The whole situation was a form of torture and she was able to stand the verbal abuse as long as he did not get more physically violent. When the time came she knew she would be able to take care of herself if she did not have to worry about little Sarah.

The train went through monotonous level lands for miles on end. The monotony was occasionally broken up by the sight of hawks floating in the sky, and sometimes there were prairie dogs popping up from their burrows and looking around. Sometimes a wolf or a fox was visible from the train. Jack rabbits seemed to be plentiful. Sometimes there would be herds of cattle or a few horses, but mostly the scenery wasn't anything to keep a persons attention for very long. The train was traveling through mile after mile of flat farmland planted in various crops of grains and corn or just grassland where herds of cattle were grazing. Evidently parts of the country was used to maintain dairies. Then when they were finally going over the higher mountains the train began to climb in earnest and the monotony was broken by a different terrain with herds of deer and other animals who were not frightened by civilization.

After several more hours on the train the skies were getting darker and darker. There was thick lightening flashing to light up the sky. The weather was also turning colder. They were just starting to leave the mountains and approaching towards some flatlands again. They only had one more mountain range to go through before reaching areas where there were farms and rolling hills. Pretty soon the rain was coming down hard with big flashes of lightening. Everyone seemed to be getting worried about the water rising in the streams. The wind was whistling and seeping through cracks in the seams around the windows. Occasionally there were flurries of snow mixed with the rain. Soon the passengers noted the train seemed to be going slower and slower. About this time the conductor informed the passengers the train was stopping at the next town due to flooding. The bridge over Tiger Creek was washed out. Informed that this delay could take up to a week to make repairs, they would have to either wait over while the bridge was being repaired or find another way to continue their journey. Being there was no public transportation out of the next town, if they wished to go on, their choice was to hire someone who lived there to take them by other means or they could go with a freight wagon that went where there were no trains or passenger facilities. The conductor also notified everyone that the freight wagon was truly built only for freight and if they took that route it would be without much comfort as to conditions for traveling. He could only recommend this if they were truly in a hurry to get to their destination. There was a boarding house in the town where they could stay while the bridge was being replaced if that was what anyone preferred.

Jackson decided they would go on with a freight wagon, the only thing available. The route of the freight wagon was still over another mountain pass. The freight wagon was not very comfortable, especially for someone with a baby. It would be a hard and cold ride for all as the wagon was only a box-like contraption with a canvas covering. Built to carry freight, it would be tough riding. Considering little Sarah and her state of health, Martha wanted to stay with the other train passengers, but Jackson could not be convinced. The fact the cold ride would not be well for a sick baby did not matter in the least to Jackson. He still would not tell Martha what his destination was. She could not figure out why he was so secretive about where they were going to end up, but she was afraid to arouse his temper by asking or insisting to know just what his plan was for them.

Another passenger decided she would also continue on instead of waiting for the repairs. This lady seemed to be quite nervous and it turned out she had an infant with her, a little boy she called Bobby. The two women introduced themselves to each other. The newest acquaintance was Helen Mason. When the two women were together they found out the two infants were exactly the same age and Helen was taking her son to a place near Mesa Ridge in the southern part of Idaho to give him up to his father. She felt she could not take care of an infant because she did not want to be tied down to caring for him, and that she had not wanted a baby in the first place. Her husband was a good man, but she did not want to live where he lived. He owned a small farm not far from the town, but she did not want to put up with the inconveniences. While the town was not far away, it was too rural for her. There was no inside plumbing, and although her husband might eventually fix everything up to be more convenient, she just did not want to put up with the inconvenience of everything now. She had really married him without thinking or considering how living conditions would be like. When she had become pregnant, she realized she did not want to be married and had left to be with her parents. She told Martha it would be up to the boy's father to find someone to raise the child, as she did not want to. Martha could not understand why a woman would feel the way Helen seemed to feel. It made her realize that Helen was similar to Jackson in a way, a person without loving feelings for family or others. It really seemed to be more a matter of being selfish as she did not appear to be abusive, just selfish. Too bad. Martha felt sorry for little Bobby, and hoped everything would work out for this little infant, and also for his father, whoever he was. It seems there were too many people without love of family. She was glad it was not her. If she ever had a chance, she would sure love this little boy, but gave it no further thought at the time.

Helen did care enough about the baby to take him to his father. When Jackson overheard Helen telling Martha she was going to Mesa Ridge, it upset Jackson, but it did not sink in to Martha's thoughts at the time and it was several years later that Martha would vaguely remember about this incident. It was at the mention of Mesa Ridge when Martha and Helen were getting nicely acquainted that Jackson ordered Martha to not get too excited about having a friend. Jackson was still showing his true colors, still showing his abusive ways. He did his threats in such a way that it was not noticeable to anyone else around them. He was quite clever about it.

The wagon was moving slow, it was miserable to ride in, and they had been on the road for several hours. With rain washing down like small creeks carrying debris from the hillside, it was worrying to the teamster driving the wagon. The passengers were getting restless and obviously worried at the sight of streams coming off the hillside. The horses were nervous and very skittish at the sight of rocks suddenly coming down into the roadway. Then, suddenly and with a terrible roar, the mountainside came down toward them. It was an avalanche of mud and rocks and water. The rain had loosened the earth so it could no longer hold up. When the avalanche came down there was the most loud and frightening roar any of them had ever heard. If the mud didn't cover them, they would be crushed by the rocks. There was no way they could avoid this avalanche. They were definitely right in the path of the sliding mountain of earth, rocks, and water. Everything happened so fast it would be a real miracle if anything escaped this mountain coming down on them. They had no warning in time to avoid it, and no way to get away from this terrible sliding mountain. They were all going to be buried here. It all happened so fast even their screams were silenced.

The horses must have been torn loose from their harness. They were frightened and instinctively they headed for their barn. By some miracle Martha and the baby boy were thrown clear of the freight wagon and its overturned load, which was partially covered by mud. It was a wonder they weren't pushed on down into the swollen creek below. With all that water running through it was like a small river. They would have drowned for sure if they had gone any further down towards the creek flowing as full as it was.

Martha heard a voice when she became conscious sometime later. It was a woman telling her that her baby was hungry and that she should nurse him. It took a minute or two before she woke up enough to understand what the woman was talking about and that she referred to the baby as "him." Her baby was a girl. The woman handed the baby to her and then informed her that the other woman was dead, and that the other woman's baby had also died in the accident along with the wagon driver and the other man in the wagon. They were cold, cold, cold and very wet and dirty. The woman had obtained some water and evidently cleaned some of the mud off of Martha and the baby. She had located some diapers among the wrecked baggage for the baby had been changed. The stranger had also found a blanket that was dry enough to help with the cold that still lingered. While the blanket helped, they were still feeling the chilly weather.

It took a while for Martha to get what had happened straightened out in her mind. Martha also began to realize that she and this little baby were the only survivors. Her husband, Jackson, her baby daughter, and Helen along with the driver of the wagon were all gone. Still stunned, she hardly knew what to do with the baby boy that belonged to Helen. It was her baby daughter that had died, not Helen's baby son.

The woman who had found them assumed that this baby was hers and insisted that she feed the baby as he was screaming because he was hungry. Martha, still groggy, said she didn't have any bottles for the baby, that he wasn't hers. That strange lady told Martha, "What does it matter. I see your breasts are leaking milk. Why can't you nurse this one." Then the woman also made a strange statement to Martha "**Who cares who milks the cow**." It had not even occurred to her that she could feed someone else's baby the same way she fed her own so after realizing the importance of what the strange woman had said, that is exactly what she proceeded to do. The starving baby knew just what to do when offered a mother's breast. He was hungry and had been screaming very loudly, and wanted to eat no matter how or who fed him. To him, eating was eating. This strange woman had referred to her right now as if she were a cow. Well a cow that was willing could feed any calf. So be it. This little calf needed milk, and right now too.

Martha instantly fell in love with this helpless little creature whose mother had just died. She could not forget her own baby, but she had known for a long time that she was going to lose her child before long and also knew she had to accept her loss and go on with her own life. This baby needed her right now and she needed him too. The baby's name was Bobby, and as he nursed at Martha's breast he would stop nursing every once in a while to look up at her and smile as if he was saying "Thank you"to Martha. For some reason, little Bobby seemed to know and appreciate what Martha was doing for him although he was only about three months old. It was uncanny. Neither knew that they would be together for the rest of their lives. Now she would have to locate this baby's father, but who was he and where did he live.? What would happen to this little boy if the father also did not want him? Martha decided "I want him and I will do everything I can for him. I swear I will find out what I have to do and do it, whatever it takes.

Chapter 3

After the Accident

As SHE CUDDLED this helpless little infant Martha started to softly croon a little song to him that her own mother used to sing. She could only remember a few words, but they were enough for him to look up at her and give her a big smile.

There's a baby in the house,
just as still as any mouse,
not a dolly, not a toy,
nothing but a big baby boy.

Bobby seemed to know that she was his best friend. They had a lot in common. Bobby had lost his mother and Martha had lost her daughter, but these two survivors were most fortunate because they now had each other.

The woman who had handed the infant to Martha

said she had to go on, but she reassured Martha that the horses would return to the way station or their home barn, and rescuers would be sent out and probably were already on their way with help. She advised Martha that her best action was to stay where she was until help arrived; This strange woman helped Martha find a couple of blankets that weren't buried in the mud, which helped them keep a bit warmer as the damp weather was chilly. Still groggy, Martha looked around, beginning to fully realize what had happened. The little boy in her arms was covered with mud, although the strange woman who had been there must have cleaned him up some. Who was that woman anyway?. She surely was not a figment of her imagination, although that was entirely possible under the circumstances. Of course it wasn't her imagination as she had talked to her. The strange woman then left them alone to wait for rescue.

A short time later Martha looked around for this woman who had been helping her and Bobby, but she had disappeared. Martha was puzzled. How strange this seemed. Where had she come from and where did she go. All Martha could identify the woman was as "the strange woman." Martha had heard the woman talk to her, had seen her help her and Bobby, but now she was nowhere around. Was it just a figment of her own imagination. How could it be. Right now she was thankful for the help she had received, even if it was a mystery that maybe would never be cleared up. Strange things had happened to others too so she would wonder if the puzzle would ever be solved.It was this woman who had strangely told her "***Who cares who milks the cow***" when she hesitated to nurse another woman's child at her own breast.

While waiting for rescue, Martha was able to clean some more of the mud off of herself, and then she rummaged through the wreckage for dry clothes for herself and the baby boy that had been pressed into her care. They needed to get dry clothes in order to keep warm as it was cold and damp. Fortunately the rain had stopped.

She grieved for the loss of her baby daughter, although there wasn't much time to do so. She just could not grieve for Jackson beyond feeling bad that he had to die in such a manner. His mean treatment of Martha just kept her from having any further feelings for him. She knew she would have left him anyway when her little daughter's life had been over. It might not have been very long as Baby Sarah was too weak to live much longer. Martha had stayed with Jackson because of the baby as she didn't know what else to do. She could take care of herself, but not with a sick infant.

There was nothing that could be done for Sarah now except to have a decent funeral service. Under the circumstances, there would be no family there to support or help Martha. She had to face everything alone, but now there was little Bobby. And so here was another small life for her to look out for—at least until his father could be found for him. This was the task that was ahead of her. She just had to do it, no matter what else went on. She absolutely could not turn that baby over to anyone else. He was so helpless and there was something about that little boy that made Martha feel that he belonged to her and she just had to take care of him. She was thinking "strange, but I feel like he is as much mine as little Sarah was. I just cannot shake that feeling. I know I should not feel that way, but for some reason I just do, I cannot help it." It also seemed as if Bobby knew that Martha was his friend.

Martha spent some time checking out her surroundings. She noted how fortunate they were that there were any survivors at all, and that her injuries were not serious even though they were painful and would leave bruises. The sun was finally coming up. She also noted that there was a beautiful rainbow in the sky. At least there was one thing better to see. Maybe it was a sign of some kind that things would eventually be better for them. It just had to be.

Martha was still unsure about whether to try to start down the road when she heard the noises of someone approaching. Relieved to see what must be the rescue party, she could finally relax and begin to think of what had happened and what she was going to have to do. How was she going to take care of this baby and herself? What would she do for money? Money would definitely be needed to get by. They would need food, clothes and shelter. She didn't think there would be much in the line of clothes left. She also had hoped they could be rescued by someone with an automobile so they would be a bit warmer, but with the roads so narrow and nothing but mud, she really did not have much hope for such a convenience as a car. A car over these roads would be unlikely.

Soon the search party had gathered up the bodies and asked her to identify any she knew that she could identify with some certainty. Fortunately she had inquired of Helen enough information to help temporarily. The rescuers helped her search for her husband's wallet, which revealed he was carrying five hundred dollars in cash. It seemed strange that this was all he had. Where was the money from the sale of the farm? That information would have to wait, and maybe she would never know. Any further grieving process would have to wait also. She could not bring herself to grieve over the loss of her husband. He had been too cruel to her. The baby daughter was a different matter, but life had to go on and there was this other infant to think about now. His welfare was the most important thing to take care of at this time. Attending to Bobby would keep her mind busy and help her contend with her loss and grief over Sarah.

The cash Jackson had on him would last for a while if she were careful. First she had to see to the burial of her husband and her infant daughter. Next she inquired from the freight company if they knew where Helen's destination had been to. They informed Martha she had bought the ticket to Mesa Ridge. After advising her to get help with the baby they then referred Martha to a local Justice of the Peace so she could get advice on how to proceed with her legal rights with the infant she was becoming so attached to.

Martha looked up the old judge recommended to her by the people who were on the rescue team. Friendly old Judge Mackey seemed interested in helping Martha in whatever way he could. He was concerned about both her and the baby. He gave her some papers showing she was to be his legal guardian until other arrangements could be made, or until his father could be located. He would telegraph ahead for her to the Justice of the Peace in Mesa Ridge to expect Martha and the baby, and asked them to notify little Bobby's father. They had learned that his name was Robert Mason. It was all that could be done under such circumstances and with such short notice. He felt it was in the best interests of the child to do it this way. This allowed Martha to continue on her journey after the deceased were buried. Martha could not notify the parents of Helen as they were unknown to her at the time. Helen's husband would have to attend to Helen's family. All that would have to wait until later, until she could find someone who would know what to do and who to notify. She had also seen to having a decent burial for Helen for little Bobby's sake. It was all she could do under the circumstances, as her money was running low. She had very little left to live on and to continue on to Mesa Ridge.

The local newspaper had put in an article about the accident which made news over a wide range of towns with newspapers. They described what had happened and when they put in the names of the victims they had listed the victims as Mr. and Mrs. Jackson Johnson and baby daughter, and that Mrs. Robert Mason and infant son had survived with minor injuries and would continue on to Mesa Ridge after a short time of recovering. Martha never saw this article and even was unaware that anything about the accident was sent all over the country, or that she had been listed among the deceased. Other newspapers had picked up the story with the wrong information about her. After all, this would be big news all over. By the time the news was printed, Martha had moved on. She did not know that her own family had seen it. She would write to them later as soon as she got settled somewhere to let them know what had happened and that she was all right. It would be several months later that she found out about the mix-up of names or that her family thought she had died in that accident, and that when her letters were sent, someone was intercepting them. The family was not receiving the letters, so they thought she had died with the rest of her family. Who knows if they would ever find out the truth under these circumstances.

Chapter 4

※

IN THE MEANTIME, both Martha and the infant needed to rest, so she had located a boarding house for them to stay in for a week while their bruises healed. Here she could recover from her own injuries and get acquainted with her new charge. The infant seemed to respond to Martha's attention. Martha recalled that Helen had called him Bobby. She also seemed to remember little songs her mother had sung to her and was singing them to Bobby. The room contained a rocking chair which she used and Bobby would look up at her and smile as she would sing:

Where are you going pretty bird?
Where are you going pretty bird"
I am going to my tree,
I am going to my tree
I am going to my tree, sweet May.

What have you in your little tree?
What have you in your little tree?
I have a little nest,
I have a little nest,
I have as little nest, sweet May.
What have you in your little nest?
What have you in your little nest?
I have three little eggs,
I have three little eggs
I have three little eggs, sweet May.
What will the little eggs be?
What will the little eggs be?
They'll be three little birds,
They'll be three little birds,
They'll be three little birds, sweet May.
What will the little birds do?
What will the little birds do?
They'll sing you a song,
They'll sing you a song,
They'll sing you a song, sweet May.

Her supply of money was beginning to get very low, which was causing some concern. She didn't have much more left than to buy a ticket to Mesa Ridge. Passage for an infant was free. She never did make it to Oregon. She had ended up in south central Idaho in a very small town in a community noted for its farming as well as lumber and logging industry. The community was called Mesa Ridge because of its location.

Martha had needed to get the information on where Helen had bought her ticket to. With this bit of skimpy knowledge she had obtained the name of the Justice of the Peace in Mesa Ridge from old Judge Mackey and planned to report to that Justice upon her arrival there. Of course the judge had wired ahead for her, so she could be met there.

Justice David James and his wife met her at the bus depot upon their arrival. Mrs. James was a very friendly woman and took them under her wing right away. She knew baby Robert's father. Mrs. James described him as a kind and honest man who was a very hard worker and very well liked by everyone. She knew he would be grateful to Martha for her care of his son. She also spent the time getting acquainted with Martha while waiting for Robert Mason to arrive. Mrs. James was impressed with Martha and felt that Robert Mason was fortunate that his son was being so well cared for.

When Robert Mason, Senior, arrived he thanked Martha profusely for her very kindness and help, then spoke up wondering how he could get help in caring for the child. This was the opening Martha needed to speak up that she planned on caring for him. She was attached to him already and did not want to let him go to someone else. He was like a son to her, and she really thought of him as her son. That is when she said she would move into his home and care for him there as she did not have a home of her own any longer. It was at this time Mrs. James spoke up and said it would not look proper for a young unmarried woman to live in the same house as a young unmarried man and it would cause too much gossip and could do harm to their reputations. This left all of them wondering what to do until Mrs. James seemed to get an idea. "Actually, you could get married." she said in a half joking manner. "That would solve the situation."

It came as a shock to everyone in the room to hear such an unheard of suggestion for two strangers to suddenly get married when they had never even met before. What a preposterous idea. Of course men were known to order mail order brides in the past when populations were so scattered that men and women could only meet in this way. Those marriages succeeded because there was nothing else that could be done, but there was no escape if they were cruelly treated either. That kind of marriage was risky.

They thought about it for a short time and Bob reasoned that he did not know of what else to do. Here was a baby without a mother, no one he knew who could step in to care for him, and a little assurance that this woman would do a good job of caring for his son. Bob's mother was dead and his father had gone back east to buy livestock for his farm and there was no one else he could think of. After all she was also breast feeding him as if she was the one who had given birth to him. Not every woman would breast feed someone else's baby. The woman must be a good and worthwhile person to do this. Could they take a chance—and it was a chance any way you looked at the situation.

Martha reasoned that she really loved this little baby that she had cared for and now she could not part from him. It would be like losing her daughter all over again. She would really grieve to lose this baby too. After all, this man had been described to her as kind and reliable. He surely could not be any more worse than Jackson had been. If she could put up with Jackson, surely she could put up with this Bob person under these strange circumstances. She reasoned she would put up with anything to keep this baby for herself. After all she had known Jackson for almost a year and yet he was a stranger that she did not get to know until after they were married. How could this be any more worse. This man had been described to Martha as being a kind and considerate man. They came to an agreement—they would get married for the sake of the child. They did not matter, only the child mattered. It was worth taking a chance. The woman seemed to love his son. Love of the baby was the deciding factor at this time.

Bob had noted that Martha was about five foot three, with light brown hair, pretty brown eyes, of average build for her age, which was probably about twenty one or twenty two. Bob did note that she was very good looking. She appeared to really love his son, which was very important. Her personality was bright. Under the present circumstances, what else could he do. He had to make up his mind immediately.

This young man was close to six feet tall, ordinary looking, with dark hair, brown eyes. He did seem to have a very pleasant personality, and was smiling and friendly with everyone in the room. He was probably in his mid to late twenties, of medium build and his features were quite ordinary but pleasant. He was dressed neatly in black jeans, wore a hat some would describe as a "cowboy hat." He was probably a typical ranch person. Jackson had been a fascinating, suave person with a dual personality that was magnetic and attractive to women. This young man was somehow different, but it would take time to tell whether or not getting married to this man was a mistake or not.

Of course there had been no way to make plans ahead

of time so right after the ceremony they headed for his home. His small house was not very far out of town on a dirt road. He was still using a horse and buggy. The road out to his home did not seem to justify having an automobile as it was deep with dirt and rutted tracks led down the middle. There were very few paved roads at this time anywhere in the area.

There was very little conversation on the way to the house. Neither Bob nor Martha could think of very much to say. After all they were actually strangers who had never met before. They did not have much in common other than the baby. For now, that would have to be enough.

Upon arrival, Bob helped Martha into the house, asked if she would be able to fix them some supper while he put the horses away. Before going to the barn he built a fire in the cook stove. He also lit a Coleman gasoline lantern for light. The house being in a rural area did not have indoor plumbing or electricity. Water was carried from a nearby well. Martha wasn't used to such primitive living but she knew she could survive. Her ancestors didn't even have this much. It would mean lots of hard work but she could do it. She and Bobby had a roof over their heads for which she was grateful.

Without knowing where anything was Martha was on her own to rummage in a strange kitchen to prepare a meal for a man she did not know. She was beginning to have a few doubts about whether this marriage was a wise idea, but it had been accomplished so she was bound to at least try to make the best of it. All she could do was to look around and try to find cooking utensils and locate enough food to fix a meal. She found an old high chair to set Bobby in and looked into the cupboards for whatever she could locate. Fortunately there were potatoes, and other vegetables, and some canned meat in a little pantry off the kitchen. She also found the flour and baking supplies. There were bacon drippings in a can near the stove, which she used to make biscuits and some gravy to go with the potatoes.

By the time Bob came back into the house she had a meal ready for them. He could not believe she had done all this in a strange place in such a short time. He freely complimented her on the meal she had prepared. He was thinking, "She must be a good cook and she very definitely was an efficient woman to do all of this".

After supper was over with and the dishes cleaned up, it was time for bed. It was then Martha started to worry and remember her wedding night from before. Sure this was a different marriage, but what if he expected her to perform for him and he was as mean and harsh as Jackson had been. It was at this time she started to learn the difference in the way some men treated women. Bob showed her where she could sleep and then disappeared out the door.

When he came back in she was ready for bed and shaking so hard and her teeth were chattering so loud it seemed to alarm him. He thought it was rather strange with the weather so warm that she was cold, but maybe she was sick so he located extra blankets for the bed and asked her if there was something he could do for her. She told him no, and he then announced that there was a bunkhouse that he would sleep in for that night until he could fix up another bedroom in the house. Relieved, she slept well that night. Bob didn't know she had been shaking and chattering because of fright and not cold or sickness. He had been concerned that she might be sick. Evidently he was a thoughtful type of person. Martha took note of that.

In the morning Martha woke up to the smell of bacon, and found that Bob had fixed breakfast for them. He tried to tell her where things were located and that he had to leave. It was harvest season and grain had to be cut and put away. It was a custom for everyone to help their neighbors during harvest and his crop would soon be ready also. With this, Bob left her on her own to figure things out. "I guess we won't be any worse off than before will we be, Bobby" Martha said to Bobby as he sat quietly in his high chair, looking around at his new surroundings. She noticed the condition of everything in the house. It was in bad need of a woman's touch. There was no electric line in the area and no indoor bathroom. Things were a bit primitive.

Before Bob left he had shown her where a few things were located, otherwise she was on her own to explore around. Martha noted there was a "cook shack" and root cellar nearby. In exploring the "cook shack" she noticed there was a washing machine in it. The machine was a square-tub Maytag made of aluminum, with a gasoline motor to run it. At least she would not have to scrub diapers and other clothes on a washboard. The cook shack was a separate building not far from the kitchen that was used in the summer time for cooking and canning so the house would not heat up. This was a method used for comfort during the hot summer months. She brought in water from the well, heated it on the stove and started cleaning. First came the curtains, which she washed, hung out to dry and started on everything in sight in the kitchen. When that was done she went outside and found some wild flowers and a glass jar to put them in. This would make things more pleasant Flowers always cheered things up.

Next she went out to the chicken coup, gathered some eggs, selected a rooster and proceeded to prepare him for dinner, hers, not his. She decided they would have a pie for desert. On arriving at the farm she had noticed an apple tree, so apple pie was what she baked. By supper time she had accomplished quite a bit.

When Bob came home he was surprised at the change in the place. He noticed she was all ready making the house into a comfortable home. Of course he was pleased and complimented her. He said he loved her apple pie, the best he had ever eaten. She was so happy that he seemed to like what she had done and there was no complaining on his part. She could relax and not be in dread that she would be criticized for going ahead on her own. This gave her confidence in herself like she had not had for a long time.

It was nice to have someone appreciate what she did and not be criticized for every little thing. Bob was showing her he appreciated her efforts. How wonderful this made her feel.

While Bob was gone, Martha explored around the farm whenever she was not busy with cleaning and cooking. Out in the corral she noticed a beautiful big black horse and wondered about him. Deciding to make friends with the animal, she took an apple out one day and offered it to the horse. Another time she offered him a sugar lump. At first he seemed skittish but eventually he would come to the fence when she appeared. After a while he let her pet him, and they seemed to have a conversation at times. It never occurred to Martha to say anything to Bob about the horse and Bob had assumed that Martha would not go near the horse, so that was the way things went between the horse and Martha for several weeks with horse and woman making friends day after day. The corral being quite a distance from the house it never occurred to Bob to warn Martha to stay away from the big black wild animal that he felt could be dangerous. The animal had never been ridden and everyone was a little afraid of him. No one ever found out the difference until quite a while later. Actually no one knew she had been caring for horses for years at her mother's farm before she had married Jackson. A nice surprise was in store for everyone in the future.

Chapter 5

Days went by and Martha kept on doing whatever she could to make the house as comfortable as she could manage. She was beginning to really relax, not worrying about being abused over every little thing. Her husband was busy and away almost all of the time during the day. He was slowly getting a little acquainted with his son. At least the baby was beginning to like him and his attention, which Martha noticed more and more as time went on. Bob was evidently a good father, which pleased Martha.

A lot of the time, when Bob came home he would hear her singing, either to the baby, or just to herself. Bob himself was starting to relax. He had wondered if he had acted in haste in marrying this strange woman. After all, she was unknown to him or even his neighbors and could be someone he would not want to be around. So far, she seemed to be all right and only time would tell if it would be a good thing, or an act he would regret. After all, though, he had acted in faith with the idea that he had to do it for the sake of his son. Maybe, just maybe, things would turn out the best for everyone. He had to have faith that it would. And she was probably taking just as much a chance as he had. So far, she was doing everything right. Maybe a little later he would learn something about her background and her family. He knew she was newly widowed and did wonder a bit of why she did not seem to be grieving over the loss of her husband, but did grieve over the loss of her baby daughter. She did seem to love his son very much, for which he was grateful. Time would tell if things were going to work out. If not, he could deal with it later. The way things were going so far, everything looked very good.

When Bob passed some wild flowers on his way home one evening, he picked a few and brought them to Martha. This pleased her very much. He was thoughtful, she was thinking. Once it was a bunch of wild roses that he had found.

One evening several weeks later Bob came home and asked Martha if she would like to attend a barn dance one of the neighbors was giving on Saturday night. It would give her a chance to meet the people in the neighborhood and maybe make friends with a few of them. It was to be held in an old school house no longer being used as a school but as a community center. There would be a potluck supper and music performed by friends. Some played the fiddle, others the banjo, and a few took turns at the piano. Bob played a guitar. It sounded like a lot of fun and she would look forward to being there. She might even be able to take a turn at the piano, although she had not played one for several years, but she was willing to do her part if she could. Bob suggested maybe she would sing for them. Singing was always welcome at any gathering and would break the ice with the people in the area and open up for the neighbors to want to meet her.

He wanted her to have friends and not be isolated. This was wonderful. What a change from her former life of a few months ago. Things were looking up.

This get-together with people in the neighborhood sounded like something she would enjoy. Bob informed her that the teen-agers usually took turns at minding the children during the party, and the young people themselves would mix in with the adults part of the time. She was looking forward to enjoying herself and to meeting more of her neighbors. Things were really falling into place. It was at this gathering that people were anxious to meet Martha. Of course they were curious to meet this young girl who would marry someone she had just met, and who would take on the job of caring for another woman's baby.

It also seemed strange to some that Bob would just marry someone he had not known for very long either. A few casually mentioned they thought Bob might have considered Candice Smith if he hadn't been in a hurry to marry a stranger. It seems that they remembered that Bob had kept company for a little while with Candice Smith while he was going to high school. Maybe he should have considered her. At least she was someone he had known for several years. When Helen died suddenly in that terrible accident he could have turned to Candice instead of a total stranger. Since Candice had never married she was still available. Candice kept staring and frowning at Martha during the evening but did not come near her.

During the evenings festivities, Martha met not only new neighbors, but became acquainted with most all who had known Bob for many years. Everyone liked her and greeted her with enthusiasm. Candice finally made a special effort to get Martha alone. She made it a point to say "You shouldn't have married Bob. He was mine. I'll get even with you for that." Of course Martha was shocked. When she asked Candice why she felt that way Candice viciously turned and said, "Bobby is not yours so why do you pretend that he is your baby?" Then she went on angrily saying it was strange that she would take in someone else's baby and nurse it as if it was her own when it wasn't. She even suggested it was very immoral to nurse someone else's infant when her own baby had died. Why was she forgetting her own baby. This hurt Martha's feelings at the time because it reminded her of the loss of her daughter. Of course this is what Candice had intended for the remarks to do. All Martha could then do was shrink back from Candice and hope Candice wouldn't make a scene by becoming violent and ruining the evenings festivities for everyone. Without saying anything more Candice just turned her back and walked away. Her actions were very strange. Martha was shocked and speechless. Fortunately, Candice didn't approach Martha again that evening nor did she say anything more.

When Martha asked Bob about Candice he told her he had dated Candice a few times while in high school. He was not at all impressed with her and completely forgot about her when he went to college. When he met Helen he never thought any more about Candice. He said he could not understand why she would make a statement as she did as he had not given her any reason to believe he had ever been romantically interested in her. He figured she was really only making awkward conversation and it was best if they were to forget about it. It was not until years later that they thought anything more about what Candice had said as she didn't approach Martha again. They thought it had all blown over and was something to forget.

Bob told Martha he had been informed by several people that they thought he had made a very good choice when he married her. "I heartily agree" he smiled.

Life went on and as Bob and Martha got better acquainted with each other, they became more satisfied with their arrangement. He saw that Martha was making their house into a comfortable home, that she was a hard working woman and taking very good care of his son, and that she sincerely loved the child as her own. He was feeling proud of himself, that he had made a good bargain when he married Martha and hoped she felt that she had done all right too. In fact, one evening after supper he asked her to sit on the porch with him as he wanted to talk seriously with her about something. He shyly put his arm around her shoulders and told her he was pleased with what she was doing. This was a friendly gesture that somehow she felt comfortable with. He wanted to discuss with her that she should feel free to ask him for anything she needed. Bob told her he was fairly comfortable financially but not wealthy by any means. He earned his living by raising livestock and a small amount of farming. He only asked that she not be extravagant.

It was during this time that Bob and Martha started

to talk about themselves and what life had been like with their former mates. Bob told Martha that he and Helen had met when they were in college and had been married after they had known each other for almost a year. After they graduated from college they had moved to his small farm and she was upset that they didn't have enough modern conveniences When she got pregnant, she decided she didn't want to have a baby so she left him and went to her parents. She gave birth to the baby and informed him she did not want to be tied down to a child. She would bring the baby to him and he could do whatever he wanted to do about it, but she did not want to have anything further to do with either him or this baby.

Bob said it was heart breaking that she felt that way, and he really could not understand any mother who could give up her infant so easily. He then told Martha he was happy that she had become little Bobby's mother and he was really grateful to her that she was so loving to him. Martha felt the same way. It was hard to understand how any woman could give up such an adorable child, but it was her gain to have gotten such a blessing as a son.

Martha then told Bob about her life with Jackson. She had known him for almost a year before they were married and he had surprised her by his actions the night of their wedding. He was so abusive to her, both physically and mentally. By the time she had recovered enough courage to leave him she found out she was pregnant and he hit her in the stomach, evidently trying to cause her to lose the baby. Finding she was expecting a baby, she hoped his attitude would change, but it did not. The baby was a month premature and born sickly, which did not endear either Martha or Sarah to Jackson and he kept on being abusive to her and eventually let Martha know he was selling the farm and moving west. He would not tell her where they were going and kept her away from her family and also kept on warning her not to complain to them. It was because of baby Sarah that she stayed with him, but had planned to leave him if and when little Sarah should pass away. She did not know why he was able to sell her inheritance without her signature, but it was either a combination of state laws or he forged her signature on any papers about the property. Martha said she was too terrified to question what he had done. She did not know what had happened to the money Jackson had received from the sale of the property. "Actually, Bob, it was worth losing whatever money the sale brought in to be away from his abuse. It is sad to say that, but that is the way I feel. He was mean clear through. In fact, my life itself may have been in danger." Martha told Bob. They wondered if they would ever learn what his destination had been.

Bob then said, "The night we were married, your teeth were chattering and I thought you were either sick or cold, but the night was warm. Were you cold or sick?"

"No, I was just scared to death because I was remembering the night I was married to Jackson" replied Martha. "I was really terrified of you, but I soon learned I had no reason to be."

Bob did tell Martha that he appreciated what she was doing for him and his son. He did seem to want to say more, but he also seemed to be a little intimidated yet.

By this time Martha was beginning to relax around Bob and to appreciate that he was a good man and was not the type to be abusive to her. It was possible that she could eventually fall in love with him. If they would always be good to each other everything would work out for them. They were on good footing for a good marriage and given time they might even realize they loved each other a great deal.

While looking forward to another forthcoming barn dance party, Martha started to worry about what she would wear. She knew she would not need to dress very fancy, but her wardrobe was very limited. She had lost the majority of her clothes in the landslide and had been making do with what little she did have on hand. It was about this time that Bob asked her if she would like to go to town early on the day of the dance and maybe she could find a new dress to wear. He was thoughtful, and she was delighted, and on that day they left early enough to give her time to shop at the only store in town. She quickly found a simple dress with a pretty lace collar. It seemed to be right for the occasion. Bob paid for the dress and then handed her some money to get whatever else she wanted or needed. He did not limit her on what she could spend of it nor did he tell her what she had to get. She only had to do what she thought was best.

In the store, Martha met the storekeeper and his family who met her with a warm smile and friendly greeting. They were glad to have Martha as a new neighbor, and would she come visit them at their home whenever she could. Martha returned the invitation.

Just about this time another customer came into the store and remarked about the sky getting darker and maybe a storm was brewing. They would remember this later.

The party gathered at the community center and in about an hour the food was set up and everyone came to help themselves. There was a nice variety of delicious dishes and plenty of it so no one would possibly go hungry. There had to be a lot of good cooks in the area, and they were generous in the amount of food they brought. Then the music started and they all gathered for the waltzes first and after that they paired up for a square dance.

There was plenty of time between dances for everyone to visit so Martha was able to get acquainted with many of her neighbors. The younger children romped around the floor and laughed and were evidently having a very good time. They eventually got too tired to keep awake and ended up crawling behind the heater to fall asleep. When Martha agreed to sing it was a delight to everyone who had come and Bob was plenty proud of her. It was very evident all were having a good time.

Strangely, Candace Smith was at the party and kept glaring at Martha, but never even approached her to say hello or anything else. It was obvious to Martha that the girl seemed to be disturbed about her in some way. Candace never said another word to her about Bob at this gathering, so Martha did not pay much attention about this situation at the time and forgot about it.

Chapter 6

The Storm Approaches

THE PARTY WENT on for several hours until someone came in and demanded their attention. The weather had suddenly turned into a flash flood and everyone was advised to stay with someone in town as some of the roads had been washed out and it would be dangerous to try to go home in the dark under the circumstances. Bob and Martha did not have anyone in town to stay with so they went to the boarding house to get a room. The proprietor informed them there was only one small room left with a small bed in it, but they could maybe one of them sleep on the floor on some blankets if they could put up with it. They also did have a crib for the baby, but that was all that was available. There was no choice but to accept what was available under the circumstances, but it was a bit discouraging to have one of them have to sleep on the floor.

They were not prepared to stay over night, did not have night clothes with them, but they decided to make the best of the situation and went upstairs and put the baby to bed, then when Bob said Martha could have the bed and he would sleep on the floor, Martha said "I have a better idea" and pulled the mattress off the bed onto the floor, spread the covers on the mattress and said, "Now there is room for the both of us""If we fall on the floor, it won't be far." With that she turned out the light, climbed into bed, and indicated for Bob to join her. Bob was surprised but too astonished to refuse.

After they got into the bed it was Bob who said, "Hey, you're plumb naked." Martha answered "I don't have fresh clothes for tomorrow and I don't want to sleep in them tonight and have to wear them again tomorrow."For the first time in their marriage, they shared the same bed. They were awake and talking for several hours after that. It was the first time they had had a chance to get really acquainted and they made the most of it.

Bob finally had the courage to tell Martha "I love you. In fact I fell in love with you quite a while ago, but was afraid you would reject me so I hesitated to tell you. I believe now is a very good time and I hope you will also learn to love me some day."

With this all Martha could say was, "We have both wasted time then, because I knew I had fallen in love with you about the time we went to the first barn dance."

They talked for several hours and then slept well the rest of that night and the smallness of the bed did not matter. He never had to sleep in the bunkhouse after that.

Before leaving town the next morning, one of Bob's

cousins greeted him with the news that they had heard that his father had met a widow on his cattle buying trip and that he had gotten married. As soon as they sold her farm, they would be heading home and his father would be bringing his new bride with him. Bob was really surprised as his father had never seemed to be interested in anyone after his mother had died and now he was bringing a wife home. He had been after buying cattle to restock his ranch.

There would be several family surprises. Both he and his father had been married about the same time and neither one knew about the other one ahead of time. Lots of surprises were in store for this family it seemed.

In the evenings Bob would stop and pick wild flowers and bring them to Martha. Then he would ask her if there was anything he could help her with and he was always very pleasant with her. Bob was becoming more dear to her all the time. She knew she was really very much in love and that Bob was a true man with morals.

Harvesting time was getting near the end and Bob was sometimes having to stay over night due to the distance home. Then late one afternoon while Martha was home alone, there was a knock on the door and when Martha answered the visitors were two young boys about ten and twelve. They told her "My mom is sick and she can't feed the baby and the baby is hungry. Can we have some milk and maybe the baby can drink it." Martha asked them where the baby was and when they said she was nearby she told them to bring the baby and their mother into the house. When Martha saw them the mother appeared to be very ill and they were all very hungry. The little girl was lustily screaming as all babies do when hungry.

The mother explained what the matter was with them. They had been at home when two men appeared at their small cabin and demanded all their money. Their father told them they did not have any money and these men shot him and killed him, took their small herd of cattle and their food and told them they were lucky he didn't shoot them too. Then these robbers burned their cabin and left the family to fend for themselves the best they could, with the threat to kill them also if they reported them or followed them.

Undoubtedly these robbers must have thought they would perish without them being the ones to kill this family. After all they were a long way from any type of help and there were no close neighbors for them to turn to. These men were evidently very sadistic.

The family had started walking and had come several miles and could go no further. They were too tired and too hungry and now their mother was sick, probably from hunger. Without food for herself, she was unable to produce milk for her infant, and along with the trauma of the robbery and murder of her husband she was tired and ill.

When Martha asked the children if they had a bottle for the baby, they informed her that this baby was a "titty" baby and did not know how to drink from a cup or bottle.

Since this baby was not a bottle baby, Martha had no way to feed the little girl except the way she fed her adopted son, and she proceeded to do so. Babies who were used to being nursed by a mother were sometimes unable to drink from a cup, and even if Martha had a bottle to use, the baby might refuse it.

She thought, "This is getting to be a habit it seems, but it is fortunate I am able to do it. This baby has to be fed, no matter how it is done. I guess it is like that strange woman who helped me at the scene of the wagon accident had said, I really was like a cow who fed her calves. Oh well, **"Who cares who milks the cow"** as the woman had exclaimed to me at that time. I can do it again. Little calf, let's eat."

Martha fed the two boys and their mother, then put the mother to bed, and had the boys go to the bunkhouse to sleep. By morning everything should be better. The problem was in the morning what could this family do with no place to go and no food either. All Martha could do was help them the best she could by feeding them and giving them shelter until something could be done for them.

Martha asked the family what their names were and the older boy told her his name was Ray Raymond, his brother was Michael but they called him Mike, and his mother's name was Annabelle. His baby sister's name was Mary.

By morning Annabelle was better and could nurse her own baby. This family had been without food for three days and the mother could no longer supply milk on an empty stomach. Annabelle was responding to the supply of food and the full night's rest and being ordinarily a strong healthy woman, she was recovering very quickly.

Now Martha was in a quandary. Would Bob be upset at her for taking this family in? What was going to happen to them, and what could she do for them. Would Bob be like Jackson would have been. She was wondering and worrying, afraid for what he would say. She was still sometimes having to learn that Bob was not like Jackson.

That evening when Bob got home all was quiet and the new family was in the bunkhouse when he arrived so he did not see them. When he came into the house he complimented Martha about how nice it was to come home and find the barn all cleaned out and the animals taken care of. This is when Martha spoke up and told him she was not the one who had done all the work.

"What do you mean? It sure didn't get done all by itself."

Shaking visibly Martha proceeded to tell him what had happened. Instead of scolding her, he told her she had done what she should have, and that he would try to see what could be done for them. They were welcome to stay. What a relief. There sure was a big difference in the way Bob took the information and the way Jackson would have. Martha was really learning how different this husband was from the first one. This Raymond family could stay and help all they wanted if the barn was an example of what they were willing to do. In the days ahead they were busy with planting a garden and anything they could see to help out. It would be a very long time before Martha ever saw Bob lose his temper. He was a mild mannered man who was calm and easily pleased.

One afternoon Martha went out to the root cellar to get some supplies and saw a rat running behind her canned fruit. She immediately thought "I'm going to get that rodent if I have to shoot through all the fruit jars" The jars of peaches were stacked six deep on the shelf. Martha ran back into the house and grabbed the 22 rifle and went back out to the cellar to get that bugger. She took aim and got him. Not a jar of fruit was broken. She was kind of proud of herself. No more rat.

Another time she was outside hanging up clothes on the clothesline when a chicken hawk swooped down at her feet and picked up a baby chicken before she even saw the bird. Again, Martha ran into the house and grabbed the 22 rifle and went outside just in time for the hawk to swoop down again and grab another baby chick. She took a shot at the hawk, but she wasn't able to do anything to hit the swift bird. The shot did seem to scare the hawk away from the rest of the chicks, although the bird probably got all he intended to get that time. Hopefully he would not return. Of course, Martha was really mad at losing two of her chicks to that robbing bird. He sure had a nerve coming right down next to her feet. "I hate chicken hawks" was her only comment at the time.

One day one of the boys came in to Martha all excited and upset. He said he had seen the men who had killed their father down the road and he was afraid they would come here, and they were in danger again. Martha had the older boy, Ray, run to a neighbor and let them know about the robbers, warning him to stay out of their sight. Maybe the neighbor would keep track of them or send for the sheriff. Raymond returned with a message from the neighbor that they were sending for the sheriff and they would be right over fully armed until the danger was over. Martha had everyone come into the house and they were to stay in until all danger was past. Martha also had a shotgun ready in case she would have to use it. Hopefully this would not be necessary, but she was prepared just in case. Bob did have guns in the house as most ranch men had.

One of the neighbors came with his son and said they would stay until Bob got home or the sheriff had arrested the bad guys. Still everyone was on edge for hours. Under the circumstances time seemed to crawl real slow. Suddenly there was a scream and one of the kids came running into the house. Tension was high because of bad guys being in the area. There was instant alarm when they heard the kids scream. When asked what was wrong the child was crying "there was a rooster in the outhouse and I sat on him." Of course this broke some of the tension as everyone laughed, although the child didn't think it was so funny. Evidently the outhouse door had been left open and the rooster had decided to go to roost in the building.

About sundown Bob arrived home and was able to give them the good news. He had seen the sheriff and it seems these same bad guys were wanted elsewhere and the sheriff and a posse had been out hunting them all day. The fact that Raymond had seen them gave the sheriff the clue as to where to find them and he had picked them up a short time ago. He evidently took them by surprise so they were not able to put up a fight. They did try to run, but the posse was too much for them. They were now locked up in a well guarded jailhouse.

Bob also noted the guns maybe should be secured because of the children around. He hadn't needed to put them away before because he was the only one around, but now it would be a good idea to not tempt young hands. They should only be available to him and to Martha so he locked them away from temptation. Curious kids sometimes mistook firearms like they were toys and would try to play with them. They would not want to have any mishaps of any kind when they could be prevented by the simple act of locking them up. One neighbor had lost a child the year before because of guns carelessly left within the reach of curious children. So all guns were immediately put into a locked cabinet with access only to adults with a key.

All this problem would bring everyone's attention in the area that a telephone was badly needed. It was time to see about getting something done to have a phone line installed. There was always a need in situations like this and also when anyone might need a doctor lives could depend on getting help quickly. Maybe a few more modern conveniences should be brought to the area. Electricity for the homes was no longer a luxury but it had become more than a convenience. It was time to bring all this to the attention of everyone who lived here. Bob decided he would call for a meeting of all his neighbors and see if they could get both telephone service and electric service, too. A lot of people did not know how nice it would be to have both conveniences so it was time to see what could be done about bringing these things into their homes.

Before his neighbor went home, Bob discussed the possibility of calling a meeting to discuss telephones and electricity and they both agreed it would be a good idea and they would both work on it.

What if Raymond had not been able to run to the neighbor when the outlaws were in the neighborhood. This should convince everyone that telephones and electricity were needed, and that they were not a luxury.

Between Bob and his neighbor they did contact everyone and explained they would look into upgrading the whole area to everyone's advantage. It might take some time to get everything worked out. They would have to look into the cost and whether enough volunteers were available to get the job done.

The first thing this group did was contact the forest service to find out if they could get help with a telephone line. They then had to locate telephones that would work. Also, there was a minimum number of people who had to subscribe to get any results. It took a few months to get everything in order. They would have to supply the telephone poles, and with everyone who could help, they cut all the needed poles and delivered them to where each one was to be installed. Some men cut the poles, others peeled the bark off of them, and others did the delivery. The women furnished the meals. If anyone could not afford the cost of wiring the houses, there was always someone who could do the wiring without charge. They got enough people to help that they made short work of getting the job done. Those who got telephones agreed to let some who could not manage to get telephones use the phones when they needed to. There was good cooperation. They were able to get phones on their wall, the kind that required a battery and all the rings would ring in each home—like one long ring and two short rings, or two long rings and one short ring. Each party had a different ring, and that was how you could tell who was being called. There had to be cooperation and occasionally there would be someone who would listen in on a call, but for the most part there was good cooperation, which there had to be with twenty parties on one line. It did work out for years that way until an improvement in telephones became available.

About the time the phones were installed at the last home, the electric company agreed to come in with an electric line, but they had to have everyone sign up to guarantee they would have electricity installed in every home over a certain distance.

Of course, there was one party who said they had never had electric lights and they could do without electric lights now also. This caused a dilemma as everyone else wanted the convenience of what electricity could do for them. The electric company would bring in the line, but everyone would have to do their own wiring at their own expense. All agreed except the one party. What could they do about that. The neighborhood committee finally thought of the solution. They would wire the house for the man and pay his minimum required fee for a year if he would consent to have it done. This was all the electric company required of the group, and under those circumstances he agreed.

They all got their electricity. They had lights, they could get electric washing machines, and refrigerators and could get electric pumps to get water into the house. What a great improvement this brought to this community. The women were especially happy about the new conveniences the electric line would bring for them. No more carrying water, no more struggling to get a gas engine to run their washing machine, if they even had a gas powered washing machine. By getting water pumped into the house it also made it possible to put indoor plumbing inside. No more having to run outside to go to the outhouse. A light could even be put outside the house so they could see at night so much better than by lantern light. What a wonderful invention.

Chapter 7

❖

Martha's Brother Appears

AFTER ALL WAS settled down, Bob informed Martha that he had met a young man in town who was looking for his sister's grave. His family had read in their local newspaper that her whole family had been killed in a tragic accident. He had found his brother-in-law's grave and his niece's grave but not where his sister might be. After inquiring about town he was told by someone that you might know something about the accident and would be able to help him find where his sister was buried.

"Since he wants to talk to you. I invited him to come for lunch tomorrow, if you don't mind". As this young man had come by horseback, he wanted to stay overnight in town at the boarding house so he could clean up, shave and get a haircut. Bob said he had asked him why he had come all that way by horseback instead of driving a car. The young man told Bob since the highway's were so rough and he also wanted to see the country first hand anyway it was just something he had to do. The horse needed a good workout and he could take his time exploring the country at the same time.

Bob continued, "The only accident I know of where anyone was killed was the one you were in. You know it almost seems like he might be looking for you. You have been writing to your family regularly and so it must be someone else. Sure strange the way things happen sometimes. It must be a sad thing for him to be on such a strange mission."

"This young man also mentioned that his mother and her new husband were going to be arriving here in a few weeks. Seems his mother met a rancher from Mesa Ridge and they got married and were on their way here. I am beginning to put two and two together and think we are in for a few surprises. Maybe we will find out tomorrow." This was all Bob said. There were too many co-incidences so he didn't say anything more. They would find out more from the young man when he arrived. Bob would not be home until evening, but Martha was very capable of handling this by herself. He didn't mention the fact that he had heard that his own father had married a widow and this stranger's mother was a widow and had just gotten married. He was thinking that all this had to concern Martha also. Too many things were adding up. They surely would find out more if his suspicions were right.

Around noon the next day the Raymond boys came running in to tell Martha they could see someone on horseback coming up the road. She kept on fixing lunch and paid no attention until she heard footsteps on the porch. Imagine how both Martha and the visitor were surprised when she opened the door. The man at the door was her brother, Don.

"I thought you were dead" he exclaimed. "We read your names in the paper and never heard from you.after you left."

"But I wrote quite often" she replied.

"We never got any letters." answered Don.

"*Hadn't Bob mailed them?*" was what she was thinking. "But no, *I mailed several of them myself* and Bob was not the kind of person who would keep from sending my mail." The mystery would not be solved for quite a while. Why hadn't they received any letters from her? The U. S. Post Office was known to be very reliable. Something was very wrong.

"If the family did not get any of my letters, no wonder I did not hear from them myself, and also they believed me dead so why would they write. There is something very wrong. I had put the required two cents postage on all the envelopes."

Before Martha had finished preparing lunch and they sat down to eat, Don asked Martha if the pretty lady he had seen outside was Bob's sister. Martha laughed and said to her brother "No, she is just a friend, and would you like to meet her?" This was something new, her brother noticing a lady like he did. He never paid any attention to any of the women he was acquainted with back home.

Then at last Don noticed the children and said "Maybe her husband would not like me to be so admiring of his wife." Martha smiled at him and informed him she was a widow. Don smiled and did not say any more.

After they caught up on the family news, Don

informed her about their mother marrying and selling the farm. Now she was coming to live on her husband's farm which was not far from here. When he told her that the name of the man her mother had married was John Mason she was shocked. Surprise!!! of surprises.

Martha said incredulously, "John Mason. That is the name of Bob's father. He has a farm not far from here."

Her mother had married Martha's father-in-law. Martha had never met him. What a coincidence. Evidently father and son had married mother and daughter. How was this going to work out. Martha just hoped that her father-in-law was as nice a person as her husband had turned out to be. Don said he was very personable and everyone seemed to like him, but only time could tell. Their mother seemed to be very happy.

Don told Martha he was looking to settle down and would be wanting a place to buy. He figured it was time he got married and started raising a family while he was young enough to enjoy having children around him. So this is why he was noticing the pretty woman he had seen outside. But would he want a woman who already had three children, two of them nearly teen-agers and one still a baby. She also would be a couple of years older than him. Sometimes though this small an age difference would not matter. Time would tell. Don was twenty-five years old. Annabelle was probably around the age of twenty-eight. She had probably been sixteen when she had Raymond. She had married at the age of fourteen. Evidently a custom where she had been raised.

What Martha could tell Don about Annabelle was not much, except she had observed how well she cared for her family, and how hard she and her sons took charge of chores around this place. Her personality was pleasant. But whatever came of their meeting, it would be up to her brother and Annabelle, and also whether her sons would accept Don into the family. They had evidently been very close to their father and it had not been very long since he had been murdered. They were probably still in shock. You never can tell how children react to a new person coming into their home. Don would have to overcome any of those problems if anything ever came of their meeting. That was up to Don though, so Martha dismissed it from her mind, at least for the time being.

Everyone might eventually learn more about what happened to Annabelle Raymond's husband at a later date, when it would be easier to talk about it. In the meantime it was very obvious to Martha that her brother, Don, was very attracted to Annabelle. It would be up to Annabelle to tell Don about her husband being murdered.

Martha's knowledge was skimpy and she felt the trauma might hurt too much for Annabelle to talk about what had happened so she had never asked her about it Some day she might tell all of them more details of what had occurred.

Chapter 8

❖

They Are Offered A New Home

ONE EVENING SEVERAL weeks later they had a neighbor, Frank Smithson, come visiting. He had met Martha and Bob at the barn dance and seemed to like them very much. He said he had decided it was time he sold his farm and got someone else to take care of it and he wondered if Bob would be interested in buying his place if he made them a good deal. Bob had to think it over as he could not manage his place and another one too, but decided he and Martha could at least look the place over before deciding. They would be able to check it out the next week. Bob did not flatly turn it down, but thought he should look into it, even if there wasn't much chance that he could handle another place. He would have to think very carefully about the financial end of any deal.

The following Sunday morning Bob asked Martha to fix up a lunch for the next day and they would travel over to Frank's place and look it over. There was a short-cut over the mountain that would save them at least two hours of travel time if they went horseback instead of by wagon. They could make a fun day out of the trip. The farm was not far away but there was a ravine they could avoid if they went over the hill instead of by the road. They would go by horseback.

That afternoon the sky clouded up, threatening rain. By evening at dark, there came the jagged streaks of lightening. Clouds had moved across the sky and the smell of rain was heavy in the air. They began to wonder if they would be able to go over to Frank's place to look it over after all. It would be useless if it was raining. Just before dawn the next morning it had rained very hard, but it soon started to clear up and the sun was peeking over the horizon, so they decided they could go even if the ground was damp. By going over the mountain they would not have to wade through mud. All they would have to do was dress according to the weather. Although the sun was peeking out there were still plenty of thick black clouds that sometimes covered the sun. A cold damp wind was rushing down the mountainside but barring rain, they decided to go ahead anyway. By dressing warmly they would be comfortable, and it would probably warm up soon also. If they did not go today, they didn't know when they would be able to make it.

Later that morning Bob went to saddle up the horses, only to find one had become lame. When he got back to the house from the barn he told Martha they would have to take the wagon and go the long way around because of the lame horse. When Martha asked Bob which horse was lame and he told her it was Barney she said "Wait a minute" and she rushed out to the barn. In about 10 minutes she returned leading a beautiful black horse. When Bob saw who she was leading, he gasped in surprise and alarm. "That's Lightening" he exclaimed. "He's never been ridden, and he's as wild as they come In fact, I'm surprised you could even lead him. No one has ever been able to lead him, let alone ride that devil." It was then that Martha broke the news to Bob that "I've been riding him for several months."

Bob was so surprised he was at a loss for words. He could only gasp, "What do you mean, you've been riding him for several months? No one has been able to get a saddle on that devilish nag, and I was about to sell him for use at the rodeo, or whatever they do with such wild horses at the auction." Bob gasped, "You say you have been riding him. How did you break him? No one else has been able to do it."

Martha innocently said, "I just made friends with him, talked to him, fed him am apple and a bit of sugar and gradually put a saddle on him. He balked a little, but got over it eventually and let me mount him one day and I've been riding him ever since."

Bob muttered something like "I can't believe it. That woman is amazing. I can't believe she tamed that devil." With that Bob and Martha and little Bobby started over the mountain to Frank's place. They had dressed warmly as the weather was still damp and a bit chilly. There was still some wind whistling down the side of the mountain through the spruce trees, but it did look like the weather was clearing up.

The trip over was beautiful. There were different species of trees. Martha had Bob identify what kinds some of them were. There were a lot of fir trees, with pine and tamarack and even some oak mixed in among them. The blue spruce were very pretty.

Martha called the sighing of the wind in the trees to Bob's attention. She said it sounded like music to her. "*Gentle music that I could listen to all day.*"

As Bob and Martha passed an old abandoned farm on the way to look at Frank's place, Bob mentioned that there was an old log house way back on the property. Bob told her the cabin was quite large, but probably well deteriorated by now as it had been over thirty years since anyone had lived there. He had heard there was probably only a few heirs left as there had been an inherited illness that ran in the family and most died quite young. Those that did not die young were not related by blood, but somehow only the ones they married lived a long life. There couldn't be many left any more. Too bad the place was empty. It had started out to be quite a nice place, but something had happened to the older ones and the younger ones didn't seem to take any interest in it.

The road up to the property was now overgrown with trees and brush, but could be cleared up with a lot of work. If the right person ever owned it, this ranch could be made into quite a nice place. A new road would have to be built, but with the right people it would work out well. The place was worth fixing up, but it would take a lot of labor, actually more work than money to do it. Maybe some day someone will take an interest in this old place. It could be a really nice home for the right people. It was then that Martha jokingly made the remark, "This place reminds me of my uncle Curtis, mother's brother.

This is just the right kind of property he would take an interest in"

Bob's great grandmother on his mother's side of the family was related in some way but he didn't know just how they were related, but probably it was through marriage. He did not know who owned the place now, but he heard that somehow it had never been probated after the last survivor known had died and it was probably a problem that it would take a "Philadelphia Lawyer" to straighten out some day. "There must be quite a tangle of heirs involved after this length of time. At least I have never heard of anyone being involved in this place since I was just a little kid. Someone must have been paying the taxes though or the county would have claimed it by now."

"I kind of remember that their names were Noland or Norland or something like that. I remember someone saying their kids had been teased about their names being "no land." That sounds like something kids would do. There were no kids when I was young—only adults then. Really, this place was probably beautiful at one time. Just look at all the fruit trees here. Someone did a lot of work on it".

"'Noland' sounds a little like the name I heard Jackson say was the name of his great aunt or some other relative. He seldom said anything about his relatives. Funny I should think of something like that. It was just something that flashed into my mind. Oh well, it is not important." Martha didn't know it would become very important a few years later.

In one area there was an old abandoned orchard that someone had planted many years ago. Martha was thinking about how nice it would be if the orchard had been taken care of, how people could enjoy the fruit from the trees. The original owner had made up some kind of an irrigation system that still kept the fruit trees alive, but they were in need of being pruned. The fruit on these trees was good, but always seemed to go to waste. The place had been abandoned for so many years that for the most part it was forgotten. It seems someone had really cared for the place at one time, but had given up. Most of the buildings were falling down and rotting. Someone had evidently had a lot of good hopes for the place. The old buildings were built of logs and the inside of the logs were hand hewn. It was too bad they were not kept up. Things like that make you wonder how people lived in the past and what happened to them.

With a lot of work the place could be made into a nice home. It was located so far back in the woods and off the main thoroughfare that most young people would not see the possibility of the place, figuring it was too much work. Seems a shame in a way. Now with the advent of automobiles making travel a little more convenient maybe some day someone will come along and develop this place into a nice home—it will take an awful lot of work though. There are a lot of possibilities here. It will take someone with a lot of patience and someone willing to put the work into it that it needs. Actually it would probably need more work than money. A big snowstorm one year had caused the roof of the barn to cave in. The rest of the building was strong.

"I have not seen the old log cabin for quite a number of years. It was built strong although the passing years have probably taken its toll on it, especially the roof. I imagine the log walls are still standing though. Maybe some day someone will come along and see the possibility of this place. It would be nice to have neighbors here that would care for the area. With electricity in the neighborhood it could be brought up here without much trouble. Wouldn't that be nice, though?"

Martha laughed when Bob said it would take someone who would see the possibility of fixing this place up. She remarked "My uncle Curtis would sure like to get his hands on a piece of property like this. He would make short work of fixing it up in a hurry. He is so handy at things like that." She didn't know how prophetic this statement would be in the future. Maybe with a place like this Uncle Curtis would get married. It was something to dream about—Uncle Curtis and this place.

There seemed to be an abundance of deer. They saw dozens of rabbits, and many small chipmunks and squirrels. The squirrels were sitting up chattering at them as they went by. Martha remarked how pretty they were and that they seemed to be talking to them. "Maybe they are objecting to us disturbing their territory."

"I tried to catch a chipmunk once when I was about nine years old. I grabbed it by the tail and the tail came off in my hand. I successfully caught one once and put it in a box thinking I could tame it. The next morning it was gone. It had escaped. I never tried to capture one again. When the tail came off the one, I decided that was not very nice so I decided to let them alone after that. I enjoy seeing them out in the wild now and have no desire to keep one in captivity." explained Bob. Martha agreed with that idea.

The whole area was very interesting. Too bad it had

been abandoned. Someone had put a lot of work into the place at one time. Maybe some day someone would buy this place and fix it up. Maybe even the fruit trees could be revived with a little bit of work from someone. That could make it into a nice small home for someone just starting out in trying to own a home. Somehow Uncle Curtis kept nagging at her mind about this place. Why did it remind her of her uncle. She hadn't seen him in months.

Bob explained to Martha that this old homestead had been occupied by a family who had hopes of striking it rich with the discovery of silver. There were several places where shafts had been dug and then abandoned. There had been quite a good showing of silver in one of the mines, but when the old grandfather had died, the rest of the family gave up, lost interest in everything, and then they all drifted away. There were quite a few girls in the family and when they had married the men they married were not a bit interested in mining. It seems they had obtained the interest of a large mining company at one time but when that interest faded away, they gave up. Some day, someone else might take up an interest in developing the mine, but it is a hard proposition without having the backing of an established mining company to take over. "It's unlikely that anything will ever be done about this property at any time soon, at least as a mining claim. Maybe someone can develop it for a small starter home. I don't know of anyone who could be interested in silver mining. It might be a different thing if it was gold. For some reason, gold seems to intrigue people more."

When they came in sight of Frank's house, Martha couldn't believe what she saw. It was a large home that had at one time been quite a show place. It was showing a need for some fixing up now, but they would have to see the rest of the place to see if it was something they could manage. The price would undoubtedly be more than they could handle. It was evidently worth a lot of money, more than they could manage.

Frank greeted them warmly and invited them in. Quickly, Frank informed Bob they needed to look the property over before it got dark. There was timber and several outbuildings, which were obviously in need of attention. Frank said he had lost interest in the place when his wife had died, but there was not any expensive repairing needed, only hard work was needed. He asked Martha if she wanted to look the house over while he and Bob inspected the land, or did she want to go with them. Martha decided she could let Bob handle that part of the property without her so she stayed in the house to inspect it. It would be the house that interested Martha, and the timber and farm land that would be what Bob would be more interested in. Whatever Bob decided would be right with her. She knew he was capable of deciding what was the best thing to do.

Martha found the house had a large parlor in the front, a big dining room, kitchen and two bedrooms on the main floor and four bedrooms upstairs. There was a cellar under the house with shelves and storage for canned goods. The kitchen was large with ample cupboards. A nice pantry off the kitchen would be a delight to any wife. There was even an indoor bathroom, which she did not have at their present house. And there was a front porch with a spectacular view of the surrounding country, a wonderful place to sit in the evenings and relax. What a nice view from that porch.

This place reminded her of her grandparents place where she had spent so many happy hours as a child. If they bought such a place as this they would really have an estate to be proud of, but would their financial situation be able to afford it. What a beautiful piece of property. This property just had to be too expensive for them to handle.

From the porch Martha could see mountains in the distance, and a meadow close by with a small creek running through it. It looked like this could be made into a park-like area. She could imagine having family picnics there. It was just the right time of day to see the most gorgeous sunset she had ever seen. There were shades of red and gold and pink and grey. This porch would be a lovely place to sit during the evenings, just to watch that sunset. Who could ever get tired of such a scene. Just beyond the meadow were trees of several kinds. She could see pine trees, fir trees, poplar trees and many others. Down by the creek was a beautiful area to have family picnics and a wonderful large blue spruce that would be the envy of anyone's picnic grounds. To the left was a fruit orchard. She wondered why Frank would give up such a beautiful place as this. She had heard though that something had happened to his family, so maybe that was the reason. She would find out later. Maybe Bob knew what the matter was. Frank wasn't very old, in fact he probably wasn't any older than thirty-five. Why would he need someone to take care of him. It almost looked like it was a matter of him being lonely more than anything else. He more than likely felt he needed someone to talk to.

She had looked the house over by the time Bob and Frank returned. Frank invited Martha to give her opinion of the house and wanted to know if she thought it was big enough for her. Martha laughed and said it suited her fine for size.

But could they afford it? What price did he want for the place? Frank said he thought $3500 was a fair price for the place if they would let him stay in the cabin up the hill and would give him a meal occasionally with the family so he would not be so lonely. This was a bargain that he was offering them. Would they be able to pass it up?

Frank also said he wanted to visit relatives in California for a while and the place would deteriorate if he was gone any length of time, and he didn't know how long he would be gone. In fact he might just go there some of the time, and stay here some of the time so it would be best to sell, and if he could stay in the cabin while he was in this area he would be happy. The cabin would be a good anchor for him, give him independence yet a good place to call home. He only wanted to visit in California, he didn't want to move there.

Then he asked Martha when she expected her baby. This took both her and Bob by surprise. Bob did not know yet that she was expecting, and Martha did not think she showed yet and had not told Bob. She thought, *"I might as well tell all right now, and I hope Bob isn't mad about the way he was informed."*

"I don't know how you knew I was expecting, as I just found out for sure myself" Martha answered.

Frank said, "I just guessed. I am right though, ain't I.?

"In fact, Martha, if you will name your first girl

Margie after my wife, I will even take $500 off the price of this place. This would make it a memorial for her. She loved this house. Of course the baby would have to be a girl to do that."

Martha exclaimed, "If one of the babies is a girl, I would be glad to name her after your wife. Margie is a pretty name. You don't have to pay me to name her as a memorial in honor of your dear wife. it's a pretty name for a girl."

Martha told them then, that she was expecting twins. Bob was grinning from ear to ear. He was not mad about the strange way he found out about becoming a father, and the bonus was two babies to boot. Martha thought to herself *"I made a good deal when I married Bob" "I sure hope he feels the same way about me."*

By the time they had all seen the whole place and talked over the terms of the deal, it had gotten late and too late to go home the same day. Martha called attention to the wonderful sunset to both Bob and Frank. It was then that Frank told them he and his wife had always enjoyed that feature about the place and that the front porch made it possible to spend the evenings where it was cool. Bob told Frank he wanted to talk things over thoroughly with Martha before they decided. They would let Frank know next week just what their decision was. They would stay over night as Frank had invited them to do.

He even had a crib for Bobby, and seemed to be enjoying their company. He had been lonely since the loss of his wife. Bob would tell Martha later that evening what had happened to Frank's wife and children. He felt it would be too painful to talk about it in front of Frank at this time, and also he hesitated to tell about it because of the tragedy that Martha had been through herself with the loss of her daughter.

Martha fixed supper for Frank and for her own family. It gave her an opportunity to use the kitchen, and maybe thereby tell more if it suited her. Everything should be all right at home as her brother was there, and Annabelle was also able to take care of things so there should be nothing to worry about at home. Don could take care of the chores. Between Don and Annabelle's boys, they would see that the cow was milked and the milk taken care of. Annabelle had helped with straining the milk before, and she would see that the cloths used to strain the milk was properly cleaned. She knew that clean sanitary straining cloths was very important to keep the milk from souring.

After supper they played a game of pinochle and went to bed by ten. Martha then asked Bob what had happened to Frank's family. It seemed he was so sad. Bob informed Martha that Frank's wife Margie and their three children had gone to visit her parents in Ohio, and while there the parents house had caught on fire and all of them had perished, including her parents and his family too. Of course this reminded Martha of the loss of her daughter and Bob's wife too. Seems they were all victims of sad happenings.

Martha felt that she was fortunate that things were working out for her. The only worry right now was could they afford this place. Too bad her ex-husband Jackson had died without leaving her with the proceeds of the sale of her property. She still felt good that her life was now in a position to be happy with an adoring husband, a beautiful son and now expecting twins, which was a happy occurrence for her. She really wanted more children.

As they said their goodbyes, Frank congratulated Martha on her ability to tame the big black horse that no one else had thought could be ridden. The horse had a reputation as a real tough hombre Maybe he had just taken a liking to someone who showed love towards him, or else Martha had a knack for taming a horse. It did seem, though, that no one could yet do anything with the horse except Martha. While he was better towards other people than he used to be, he still was a stranger to anyone else. Martha was his friend and he evidently must not want any other friends, but he no longer seemed to be a dangerous animal to anyone else. Strange things sometimes happened with some animals. They took notions the same as humans did, it seems.

Bob did not indicate displeasure either over the way he found out he was to be a father again. Bob asked Martha if she was afraid of him, and she had explained how her former husband had acted when he found out she was going to have a baby. Bob then informed her to quit assuming that he would act like a madman about anything she did, but he wanted to know if she would leave him as Helen had done when she found out she was expecting a baby. Both Bob and Martha had to overcome the trauma each suffered at the hands of their former spouses, but they were slowly adjusting and as long as they were communicating everything had a chance to get straightened out.

As time went on Bob and Martha were constantly learning more and more about each other. Then Bob explained that if they would always talk things out they could really get along and be happy. Yes, he was looking forward to becoming a father again, and having twins was a bonus. Martha was happy about the coming event and no, she had no plans to leave because she was expecting a baby, but was extremely happy over it. Also she did not want to raise her son, Bobby, as an only child so everything was working out just right. She had emphasized that Bobby was her son, whom she did not want to raise as an only child.

Bob and Martha were very much in love, but old hurts kept bobbing up every once in a while for both of them. By talking things over they were able to slowly overcome the trauma these hurts had caused. They were understanding each other more and more all the time and keeping communication open is what was helping.

On the way home, Bob indicated to Martha that if she liked the place he wanted to buy it, but did not know if he could raise the money. Frank had indicated he would take payments. They would have to sell the present farm and who knows how long that would take. What could they get out of it? The price Frank was asking was really a bargain as the property was worth a great deal more. The house was what they would need if they were increasing their family. In fact the size of the house would accommodate quite a large family if they ended up with a large family.

Did Martha want a large family though? Because Helen had left him over not wanting any children, Martha had been afraid that Bob might be unhappy about having more children so they did discuss this on the way home. Talking to each other is what was making this marriage a success, and it did seem to be a success. They found out that Bob was very ecstatic over the prospect of having more children, and Martha was also happy that Bob's attitude was so good. Bob told Martha she could have all the children she wanted, that it was up to her about how many they had. Now that was settled wasn't it, that they both wanted more children and looked forward to the event.

The couple continued on the way back home and enjoyed the scenery. There were birds of many kinds, beautiful quail with crests, several deer, many squirrels and lots of rabbits running through the woods. They went past the old abandoned farm again and wondered what would eventually become of it. Someone should occupy it some day. "I still think my uncle Curtis would love this place. I don't know why I feel that way about it but this place just reminds me of my mother's brother."

They got to discuss how their family could enjoy the bigger house with the expected larger family. It would be a matter if they could make payments, which might be hard to do. The farm would have to help pay for itself and it would take a lot of hard work to make payments. A lot of planning would have to be done. The offer Frank made was almost like he was giving it to them and the bargain would be very hard to pass up. They would have to plan very carefully and would not be able to do anything unless they could sell their own place and could get enough out of it to swing the deal. Actually their place was worth $3500 in itself. It would be nice if they could sell it for that amount.

Frank's place would be ideal to raise cattle or horses or both. There was enough cleared land to raise grain and other crops they would need. They would have to figure out just how to earn more money, and ideas were beginning to form in their minds.

Besides raising cattle, there was the possibility of logging part of the timber. There were quite a few possibilities. The orchard would bring in some income if they handled it right.

His father might have enough cattle to get them started with a larger herd. There were all kinds of possibilities Now, things were getting exciting. Martha had experience with horses so maybe she could help somehow with that knowledge.

Bob expressed his feelings to Martha about how he felt about the way things had turned out between them. He told Martha "The day my son met you and the day I married you was the most fortunate days of our lives. We could not have done any better, and I love you dearly." He repeated, "There is no way possible that I could have done any better than the way things have turned out."

With tears of happiness in her eyes, Martha told Bob she felt the same way about him. She had gained a wonderful son, and also the best husband any woman could possibly have. Meeting and marrying the way they had, was very risky, but she was also very happy the way things had turned out.

Both Martha and Bob realized that at times there would be a difference of opinion between them, and it would take work and patience on the part of both of them, but with determination they would be able to work anything out. Kindness and understanding is what they would both have to work at and they knew they could do it and they were both determined that they would.

Chapter 9

✦

A Buyer For Their Place And They Open The Trunk For A Surprise

MARTHA'S BROTHER DON was getting ready to go to town a few days later and he mentioned that he was going to look for property in the area. In about the same breath he made an off-handed remark that he wished Bob's place was for sale. Bob and Martha looked at each other and started laughing. Don thought they were laughing at him until they spoke up and said their place might be for sale real soon. "We have another place in mind that we have been offered."

"Why do you want to buy a place?" they then asked Don.

"Because I have decided to get married and settle down." was his reply. "I think I will ask Annie to marry me. I like her, and if there is no trouble from her sons, I will marry her quite soon if she will have me. She seems to like me and I like her and her kids too. I get along quite well with the boys, and her little daughter has started to call me Daddy. I kind of like that, even though what started her to calling me Daddy is a mystery to me. The boys call me by my first name, but I don't object to what the baby calls me."

"I would want to wait until Mom and her husband get here." he continued. "I know we haven't known each other very long, but who has time for a long courtship these days. Let me know soon about whether or not you will be selling your place because I don't want to wait too long and I like this place. I can see that it has great potential and is about the right size for me as a place for my first home. You decide on a price and we will negotiate."

Don then informed them it was time to invest in an automobile, that as more and better roads were built and were also being improved more and more that using horses was becoming a thing of the past and would very soon become too obsolete to be practical. He then left for town.

Bob and Martha were left to discuss whether or not to go ahead and buy Frank Smithson's farm, but evidently Don's announcement most certainly was the frosting on the cake that would help them make up their minds. Really, the opportunity was too good to pass up. Here was a chance to sell their own place, and they had been offered a choice piece of property, with a good house on it and they would not only be needing a larger house, but had an unusual opportunity that seldom is ever offered to anyone. The man was practically giving the place away. The only catch was he wanted to live in one of the buildings and have an occasional meal with the family, which would be tolerable as he was not asking for room and board, but to eat with the family once in a while. He was evidently lonesome and eating with a family would be a way to help. The cabin that was livable was quite a ways from the main house, and was evidently the original one used before the larger house was built. Also he had mentioned that he was going to spend a part of his time in California visiting relatives and friends.

They only had to decide if they would be able to make the payments on it. It would be almost a tragedy if they had to pass this opportunity up. There would have to be a lot of thought about this. Frank living in the cabin should not be a problem and since he planned on sometimes going to California he probably would not even be there much. Also he was asking to have an occasional meal with the family, not be there regularly like a boarder.

Times were still booming since the war to end all wars had ended, but how long would it last. There was prohibition and some people were making moonshine and selling it. Of course they were able to sell the stuff because it was not available in stores, but the Federal government was cracking down. They would have to watch out that someone didn't sneak onto the property up in the hills and set up a still. This had happened to others. They were sure Frank wasn't one who would put up with it either. There was a lot of corn grown in the area and the best way they could get it to market was in liquid form.

Frank had told everyone that if they wanted a drink that it was their business, but it was better to buy it elsewhere, but not to make it themselves, and not on his property. "Maybe I don't agree with the government on all things, but we elected them and the majority of us need to stand by them and their laws on prohibition."

Before Don left for town, Martha asked him and Bob to bring her steamer trunk down to the house. It had been stored overhead in the bunkhouse for several months and Martha decided that now she was going to have a baby that she ought to check it out as maybe she could use some of the clothes in it or at least see what she could do with whatever was available for the future.

Seeing the trunk and knowing it contained items that had belonged to her infant daughter, she became quite sad and could not bring herself to open it right away. There were so many sad memories connected with the contents of that trunk that it was hard to have to delve into looking at what was in it, but she knew she would have to sooner or later anyway, but she would put it off until later that evening. Of course that trunk would remind her of her former husband as well as her daughter. It could not be helped. She just had to make up her mind to look into the trunk and try to forget all the tragedy it would remind her of.

Maybe Bob would help her after supper was over. Every time she would look at the trunk it was hard to keep from crying. She kept thinking also, "Why was Jackson so intent on my taking this trunk, when he wanted to sell everything else or leave it behind?" It was so hard to understand, but he had been difficult ever since the day of their wedding and this was no exception. Maybe there was something about the trunk that would explain just why he was so intent about it and nothing else of their possessions.

That evening, after supper, Bob asked Martha

whether she was ready to explore the trunk with his help, so they opened it up and started looking things over. It contained baby clothes of every description. Many hand made dresses. Beautiful knit clothes for little girls. None had been used. There were diapers, which were very usable for any baby, and shirts and other items that could be used for either boys or girls. These would all be handy for the new babies.

They had the trunk almost empty when Bob saw something odd about the bottom of the trunk and asked Martha why it was so different at the bottom. She had not noticed it before so they investigated and had quite a surprise when they discovered a false bottom had been added to the trunk. When they removed the false part, they were so surprised they could hardly stand up. No wonder Jackson had been so protective of this trunk. The mystery of where the money for Martha's inherited farm had disappeared to was solved. Neither one could hardly believe what they were seeing. There was five thousand dollars in cash hidden in the bottom of that trunk. Who would have thought to look among baby clothes for a fortune. Here it had been in storage for so many months with no knowledge of it's contents beyond baby clothes.

Martha immediately said to Bob "Now we can buy Frank's farm."

Bob's immediate answer was "I don't think so."

When Martha asked him why not he answered, "That is your money."

"But, I want it used to buy Frank's place, and we won't have to make payments." she exclaimed in surprise. Bob was adamant that it was her money, and she was just as adamant that they should use it. She was hurt and reminded Bob they were to talk things over. He insisted she was to put the money away for herself, that he did not feel right to use her inheritance and she in return asked him what better use could she put it to. She then suggested that they think it over until morning anyway and maybe they could come to some kind of an agreement. There was no sense in arguing about money. By morning they would have had time to think about what to do with this unexpected fortune. By morning the shock would also be worn off, because it was a very big shock the way it had turned out. There was no sense to argue over money so waiting until the next day would give them time to think more clearly.

This was the first big disagreement they had had since they were married a couple of years ago and they were both being stubborn. They agreed to wait until the next morning to discuss the money after thinking about it over night. They could settle down and to think more clearly about what would be best to do with this surprising and unexpected windfall, but it belonged to Martha only, according to Bob. So with that in mind, they both settled down to think things over. By morning maybe the surprise of it would be settled and they could think straight, the both of them.

Sleep did not come very easy that night, but they hoped by morning things could be straightened out. The amount of money they found was a tremendous fortune. The shock of finding so much money and so unexpectedly kept them both on edge, but both were determined the answer would be determined by morning. They would talk things over and would come to some kind of a solution. It was best to get over the shock first.

By the next morning Bob and Martha awakened after tossing and turning all night.

Both were unhappy that they had been upset with each other over the windfall they had found in the trunk. Each claimed they had a solution. Martha told Bob she was sorry it had come to such a disagreement with them, and over such a silly thing as money.

Martha told Bob "I don't want this to come between us. While I don't understand why the money cannot be used to pay for our new home, I will do whatever it takes to have us not be unhappy over it." She would compromise in any way she could.

In turn, Bob apologized to Martha and made his suggestion. "I do not feel it would be right for me to take your inheritance, but I think it could be used in a different way that would work out for both of us. What do you think of using part of that money to fix up the house any way you would like it. Another part of it could be used to buy a few cattle to start a herd. I could work at raising and increasing the herd. That way I would feel better that I had earned the money that the cattle would bring in and we could use part of the profit to pay for the farm. It would be an investment for you and we will both be earning our way."

"Yes, yes, yes!" Martha squealed in agreement.

Bob added, "At least a third of that money should be put away in case something should happen to me in the future and you would need it for some reason." They were now in agreement. They would inform Don about their decision when he returned, and by the next morning they could also inform Frank they would take him up on his offer for his farm.

Frank told Bob and Martha that he was going to spend the winter in Los Angeles with friends and relatives there, and he would be back in the spring. He was going to buy a piece of timber land on some acreage not too far from his present farm and it would be an investment and would be available if he ever decided to build on it. In the meantime what belongings he was keeping could be left in the cabin and he would have a place to stay when he was in this area. This would be satisfactory with both Bob and Martha.

They would all have a lot to do before the twins arrived to join their family. About the time the twins came along little Bobby would be two years old. Time was passing fast, and a lot was going on with this family. It looked like the family was fast growing with new in-laws and new babies.

Chapter 10

✦

WITH THE NEWS that Bob and Martha were buying Frank's place and Don was buying their place, Annabelle was wondering if she would have to move, and what was she going to do. While the bunkhouse wasn't much of a place to live, it was shelter for her and her children and she had nothing to go elsewhere with. Her sons were too young to get out and earn their own living yet. What could she do with an eight month old child and two teenage boys? It was too large a family to find a place where she could work for room and board for the whole family. Maybe Martha could make a suggestion that would help, although she hated to have to ask her for more help after all they had given her family already. What to do? It was with reluctance that she decided she would have to see if Martha could make any suggestions.

Annabelle hesitantly approached Martha with her

worry about what she was going to have to do when they moved. This startled Martha as she had not even thought about Annabelle or her family. "I'm sorry, Annabelle, but I have been so busy and absorbed in my own thoughts I did not even think about you. I am sure between all of us we can figure something out. You have become like a sister to me and we won't let you down, so let me see what we can all think of. In the meantime, don't worry too much about things. Something always turns out in the long run. We'll figure it out."

Evidently Don had not followed up on his original interest he had shown in Annabelle or she would have probably said something. Martha decided to inquire discreetly how Annabelle might think of Don. She asked Annabelle how her brother had reacted to her boys, and Annabelle told her in glowing terms how they liked him and that they had all been working together and playing games and getting acquainted. Her boys enjoyed Don's attention as they missed their father. His attention helped them overcome the loss of their father. He was making it easier on her also. She giggled when she told Martha that her little girl called him DaDa one day. She said she was a bit embarrassed over it, but that Don did not seem to mind. In fact, Don seemed to act as if little Mary was his own child. She hoped he did not mind but the baby really took to his attention, but she was wondering how her children would cope when they had to part when Bob and Martha moved over to their own new home. Martha could tell that Annabelle was feeling quite sad over the prospects of all the changes ahead.

Martha was thinking "Ho ho! So that is what his game is." "He's courting the boys first, the rascal." I know he is interested in Annabelle but he is wise enough to know that he has to win the boys over first. Win them and they will be on his side. The big lunkhead, so that's his game is it? He is wise. I sure don't need to be a matchmaker. He is doing all right on his own. I will bet Annabelle does not have a problem of where she will have to stay when we are gone. My brother can take care of himself. I bet I will have a new sister by the time we move to our new house. Good for them. I like her and I think she will make a good wife for my brother."

"Oh!! I'll bet maybe that is why Don inquired about our place. He has something up his sleeve. I really believe he is planning something. We'll just have to wait and see. I hope he doesn't wait too long."

A few hours later Ray and Michael came running up to the house and were so excited they could hardly gasp out that someone was coming up to the house. Whoever it was they were in an automobile. Not too many people in the area had automobiles yet so the unusual fact of one coming up their road, made for top excitement. This brought everyone out to the road. Who could be driving one of those machines up here? Yes, it was Don, of course. He had mentioned that people were using them more and using horses less since better roads were being built for them. It was like him to be the first in the family to get one of those modern vehicles that were rapidly replacing horses. This was especially true in the rural areas of the western states. The eastern states were more settled and had more paved roads, so cars were more common back east.

After the excitement died down a bit, Don informed them he had made arrangements to open a repair business on the edge of town to repair cars. He would also apply for a dealership so he could sell new cars. If people bought cars, they would also need to repair them sooner or later. He knew a lot about machinery and felt that since most people did not know how to fix automobiles, it would be a good business to get into right in the beginning. Now he could be quite serious about settling down. With a smirk on his face, he made the remark "Now all I have to do is find a wife and kids." "Does anyone know of someone who is available?"

With those remarks he went into the main house without further word. Everyone stood with their mouths open in wonderment. What in the world did he mean? Martha glanced at Annabelle and got to thinking to herself, "he sure is a tease. I think I know what he is up to."

Annabelle turned and headed back to the bunkhouse, looking a bit downhearted. Now she knew she would have to find another place for her and her children to live. But where could they go. For sure they would have to find a place to move to since Don had mentioned he was going to find a wife. Now there would be no place for her and her family. Just where could they go. She was almost crying as she headed back to the bunkhouse.

A few minutes later Don came out of the main house and headed towards the bunkhouse, and summoning Ray and Michael to come with him they all went to the bunkhouse together. About five minutes later the two boys came out running and shouting at the top of their lungs. "We're going to get married, we're going to get married." It seems Don had headed back into the house to pick up a ring he had hidden there a few weeks before. Annabelle had evidently said "yes"—the boys too!!!

Weeks passed and everyone was making arrangements for Martha and Bob to move over to their new home. They had been fixing the place and getting it ready to occupy the buildings. Martha had been decorating the house with paint and new curtains throughout slowly as she was getting quite large with the twins keeping her slowed down. Her health seemed to be going quite well, and everything with the babies was also not giving her any trouble. It would not be very long until her mother and her new husband would be arriving too. It would seem so odd to have her mother married to her father-in-law. What a coincidence. If her mother was happy it would be almost impossible to imagine that everything could be going so smooth for the whole family.

When Martha's mother, Jean, arrived there would be the wedding for Don and Annabelle. Everyone was going to be quite busy. Don and Annabelle planned to fix up Bob's place. They planned on adding another bedroom and an indoor bathroom to the house right away in time to have it ready for them at the time of their wedding.

There would not be much time to get everything done, but they were going to try. An electric company was coming into the area so an electric line into the farm would make it possible to have water pumped into the house from the well, and another bedroom added to the house would make it possible not to have to use the bunkhouse any more as a bedroom for the family. All was going quite well.

Now they would be looking forward to the arrival of their parents, Jean and John Mason. Martha was hoping her mother would arrive before the twins were born. Fortunately this pregnancy was not like her first. Martha didn't even have much morning sickness this time and she felt really good the whole time.

Little Bobby was walking and of course getting into mischief as all babies do. He had to be watched carefully, but Ray and Mike treated him as if he were their little brother which helped Martha tremendously as she was now getting quite large. Twins were taking up a lot of space and making it a bit difficult for Martha to get around any more. Their arrival time was getting nearer and they were hoping to finish moving before the big event. In the meantime Don was adding onto the house while Bob and Martha were still there. While Bob and Martha were working on their new place, Don was taking advantage of working on his new purchase so it would not inconvenience Martha too much while she was expecting her babies. It was beginning to look like everyone was accomplishing what they needed to do. So far everything was going quite smooth.

As usual, when neighbors need help, all that was needed was for the information to go out and there was someone ready to do what was needed. There had been a nice group who showed up to help Bob and Martha with the minor repairs that were needed around their new place and it did not take long for the painting to be accomplished also.

Of course it was always a good reason to have a party so everyone had a good time while fixing the place up for them. Then they pitched in to help them move into their newly renovated home. As if that was not enough, the neighbors decided they would also help

Don get their house ready. Of course they would have to reward everyone with another big shindig when that job was done, so there were quite a few parties planned for entertainment in the last few months before the twins were born. Helping the neighbors was always a good way to be friends and made life enjoyable with all the get-togethers. It would be someone else's turn some day to be helped. These "barn-raising" events were always looked forward to by everyone. They helped each other out and also it brought everyone together to have a lot of fun out of the event. The ladies furnished lunches at noontime, so they managed to make a big party out of it every day they worked. After the work on the house was finished there would be a big dance. Everyone always enjoyed this fellowship and looked forward to it every time.

Chapter 11

❖

Parents And Twins Arrive

JEAN AND JOHN did arrive shortly before the twins were born. This was a very happy occasion for all of them. There was quite a bit of news to catch up on from everyone. Martha informed her mother about her accident, her marriage, and all that had happened since. Jean got a chance to meet her new grandson and son-in-law, and Martha got to meet her father-in-law and they all had to figure out what their relationships now were as this included double step-parents as well as in-laws. Seems that father and son ended up marrying mother and daughter, all quite by accident that it turned out that way.

Jean and John had found out about the marriage of Martha and Robert about the same time that Don had discovered that Martha was still alive. It seems that a cousin, Rosalyn, had been jealous of Martha and her marriage to Jackson. She thought she had wanted to marry

Jackson and resented Martha to the point of stealing the letters Martha had written home. The cousin, Rosalyn, had read in the paper the obituary that was erroneous about the accident that the newspaper printed about who had died and had discovered letters from Martha and was stealing them. She read the first one Martha wrote telling the family she had survived, and decided to let the family think she had died.

It was not until Jean had married John Mason that John discovered Rosalyn was stealing the letters and when he confronted her about it she confessed what she had done and gave them Martha's letters. This is why Martha had never heard from her mother in all those months. Jean did not know what had actually happened to Martha and in turn Martha did not know her mother had met and married John Mason until many months later. Jealousy had consumed Rosalyn beyond reason. What a terrible thing she had done.

After all the excitement of getting acquainted and catching up on the family news it was time to start planning the wedding of Don Fisher and Annabelle Raymond. Before those plans could be finalized though, Martha started into labor.

As it seemed to be a bit too early for the twins to be born there was some concern about the event, so Bob sent for the mid-wife as soon as Martha had her first cramps. Fortunately, it was a good thing the mid-wife came early. It was not a false labor as it turned out and it even was not a long labor as some labors are. Everything seemed to go smoothly and the babies were born healthy even though a couple of weeks earlier than they had been expected.

There were two little girls. The first, Margie, weighed

six pounds and the second, Myrtle, was six and a half pounds. They had very strong voices and came into the world healthy and hollering very loud about ten minutes apart. Mother and babies did fine. Parents and grandparents were very proud.

When Bob saw the little girls he exclaimed, "What beautiful little girls. How will I tell them apart. They are so identical." Of course they had to have ribbons tied to their tiny wrists so they could be identified. Bob was thoroughly proud.

"This is a double blessing that I never dreamed would ever happen." he continued.

"The day Martha came into my life was the luckiest day of my life. I gained a wonderful wife and now my family has increased beyond what I could have expected. My son got a wonderful mother in the bargain. Our lives have been blessed. In fact our whole family has been blessed, from me to my father as it has turned out that Martha's mother is also a good woman for my father."

Everything was going quite well for Don and Annabelle. They had become acquainted with their neighbors and their friends were giving them engagement parties with many gifts for their new home, and were also helping them with the additions they were making. Word had spread of their impending wedding and that was all it took.

Now it was time to complete the plan for the wedding of Annabelle and Don. They had finished adding to their home. The addition consisted of another two bedrooms and a bathroom. in addition to the two bedrooms there were already in the house. This gave them ample room for their already existing family, and hopefully it would be big enough in case there was ever an additional need. The bringing in of electricity to the area had allowed them to pump water into the house from the well so they could really modernize the house.

About four months after the arrival of the twins Martha's mother was visiting her and seemed to be quiet and thoughtful. Martha finally asked her what was wrong and her mother burst out crying with the information "I'm going to have a baby. I'm too old to be having a baby. No one has babies at my age." Martha could only smile at her mother, but she seemed so serious that she knew her mother needed to express her feelings without any remarks from her.

When Jean calmed down Martha expressed the opinion that "When you think about it you will end up being very happy. You are not too old and you will probably find this is the best and happiest event of your life. You will have more time to enjoy a child, and not have the worry about your income being sufficient to support a child. Besides I will bet John is happy about being a father at his age, or have you told him yet?"

"He must have been suspicious because he did say he thought it was nice when people had children when they could afford them. He had no reason to say that unless he was trying to get me to tell him something."

"Well, Mother, do tell him, and I will bet he will be happy about it. I know you are a bit shocked to find you are expecting after all these years, but I have heard women express the opinion that they enjoyed the one that came later in life so much more than the earlier ones because they had the time to enjoy them."

"You really are not too old."

"How are you and John doing? Are you happy?"

"Oh Martha, it has been wonderful. Your father and I had a real good marriage, but while John is different from your father, he is a wonderful person and I am very happy. He treats me like a queen. We really do have a happy marriage."

Jean went on, "Thank you, Martha, I feel better all ready. I know you must be right. I'll talk to you later."

"And, Mother, I will be looking forward to a new brother or sister. I know Bob will feel the same way. Won't it be something, both Bob and I will have the same brother or sister. This will blow the minds of some other people trying to figure that out. We can have a lot of fun over that and you can bet the men will make the most of it, too."

A few months later, Jean and John became the parents of a little boy who did become the joy of his parents. In fact, they decided they would also have another child so it was no surprise that they greeted the next one a year and a half later. That second one turned out to be a girl. Martha had been right, the children born to older parents sometimes were the joy of their lives.

Time seemed to fly by. About three years later Bob and Martha added another boy to their family. In the fall Bobby would be going to school, Margie and Myrtle were active three year olds. Their home was the scene of many neighbor gatherings. Martha was well liked by her neighbors. They had purchased a few head of cattle and now that herd was increasing to the point that it was bringing in a nice income.

They finally had telephones and electricity into most of the homes throughout the whole area. With the advent of electricity they could have pumps and with pumps they could have water into the house. With water in the house, they could have indoor plumbing. Things were getting better and better all the time. With telephones they could now conduct business over the phone and it also saved many a trip to town. Relatives and neighbors could now contact each other without ever leaving the house. The whole neighborhood had flourished with the new improvements. People were moving in all around the area and the population was filling in with new homes and the roads were constantly being improved. A new school was being built closer so children would not have to be bussed so far to get an education. With paved roads the children would go to school by bus even in the winter time instead of having to use horse and buggy because of deep snow. Yes, times were changing very rapidly.

Chapter 12

One day little Bobby came home from school crying. It seems that one of the children had started teasing him that he didn't have a mother, that Martha was not his mother, she was only a step-mother, and that step-mothers didn't like step-children. They compared a step-mother to a wicked witch. Bobby was crying his heart out.

What was Martha to do? This was serious. It could cause harm to not only Bobby, but to the whole family if not taken care of. Martha got to thinking about what to tell him. Of course she never thought of him as anything but her son. He was every bit as dear to her as any of her children who had been born to her.

She would have to overcome the efforts of a bully to intimidate little Bobby.

Martha finally put her arms around Bobby and asked him: 'Tell me, what does a mother do?"

Bobby answered, while sobbing, "Mothers take care of kids."

"Don't mothers also love kids Bobby?"

"Yes," was his answer.

"Do I take care of you?"

Again it was "Yes."

"Don't you think I love you?"

"Yes"

"Well that should settle it. I take care of you, and I love you."

"The kids who teased you were bullies who were trying to make themselves seem important. All they did was talk about something they did not know anything about."

"Who is it that had been teasing you?"

"It was Candace Smith's little brother. He said his sister doesn't like you because you are not my mother."

"Honey, that explains this a lot to me. Both Candace and her brother are very much mistaken about me. You can just remember, I have loved you right from the very first time I saw you. I don't love you more than any of my other children, but I love you every bit as much. When the nice lady who gave birth to you died, I picked you up and fell in love with you right away. You were a very tiny baby when I got you and I loved you right from that very minute."

Martha continued on and Bobby was listening. "Technically I guess I could be called your step-mother according to some people, but I think of you as my son and that I am your mother in every sense of the word. Do you understand what I am saying.?"

"Yes, now I know, you are my Mama and I love you. If that bully ever says anything like that to me again, I will tell him I have the best Mama in the world and he doesn't know what he is talking about, and I'll knock his head off"

"I think that won't be necessary. Just don't pay any attention to him any more."

It never bothered Bobby again. In fact, years later, he told his sisters he had the best mama anyone could ever have, and he meant it.

After Bobby went out to play, Martha realized this was the way Candace was "getting even" with Martha for marrying Bob, when Candace had imagined that it had been her that Bob should have married. She hoped that Candace was satisfied that she had accomplished her purpose of "getting even" and would forget any further animosity towards Martha and her family. Some people just seemed to be petty and have insecure personalities. This maybe would be the end of her animosity now that she had accomplished her purpose. So far there was no real harm done.

Don had been right when he said that people would soon turn from the use of horses and would be using automobiles more and more. His repair shop was doing as well as could be expected for the times, even if they did not have many other extras. He was barely making ends meet. Like everyone else since that awful day of **October 1929** when the stock market crashed and started the depression, they had to be very careful about what they spent. They were managing by raising their own food and between Martha and Bob, and their parents, Jean and John they all helped each other by pooling their resources. They all raised gardens, shared their livestock and by all of them working together they lived comfortably. Times had gone from being exceptionally good, to being very hard. The stock market crash was affecting the whole world and the economy was very bad for most people.

Once in a while Don would be able to sell a car to someone who had survived the crash. Between him and Annabelle's sons, Don was keeping the repair shop going, but earning a living was really hard. They had gone into the depression years without a lot of debt so they did not have as much trouble as some people did.

Between a garden, raising cattle, a few chickens, and staying out of debt, both Don and Bob and John were weathering the depression years fairly well. They had enough to eat and by being careful they were able to get enough money to pay their property taxes. Their wives were able to sew their own clothing and they processed their garden and fruit each summer. They all felt quite fortunate, especially in comparison to some other folks. They could sell eggs for 12 cents a dozen for some cash and trade other items for whatever else they needed. The creamery was still buying cream to make butter, even though they were not paying very much for the cream. They could buy a huge bag of groceries for a dollar. Martha had deposited her money in a bank from the sale of her farm and which she had found in the old steamer trunk. As she had used a good size chunk of the cash to fix up the house she and Bob had purchased from Frank and had invested in livestock with another big chunk of the money, when the bank closed very fortunately she did not lose everything as a lot of people had lost. By now the farm was almost paid for and the payments had not been large which had helped out a lot. They were able to pay the taxes by selling cream, eggs, and fruit from the trees in the orchard, along with vegetables from the garden. Of course they had their own beef so they were faring much better than a lot of people, especially those who lived in the cities. The same was true for Don and Annabelle and John and Jean.

Since Martha had tamed the big black horse called Lightening, others had asked her how she had done it, but all she could tell them was that she treated the horse with love and the horse had responded,. She did have a knack with horses though and any she raised always had a buyer waiting. They were always tame and she warned everyone who purchased one of her horses that they had to be kind to the horse to get the animal to respond in kind. She had not made a large business from raising horses, but a few that came from her were always tame when they left her barn. She had a good reputation for the way she treated her animals and it always showed up with the way the animals responded.

Chapter 13

✢

Hard Times - Letters

THE FAMILIES WERE keeping their heads above water during these hard times. They could indulge in a movie occasionally, and have a 5 cent hamburger once in a while. The kids could get a nice Hershey chocolate bar for a nickel, and a bottle of creme soda or a bottle of Coca Cola pop also for a nickel. Penny candy was available whenever they went to the store. They would also buy a milk shake for a dime sometimes. While they couldn't afford too much, there were some people who had nothing so this family felt very fortunate. Some were trying to exist by selling apples or pencils on the streets of the cities, doing whatever they could to raise a nickel.

These were also the days of prohibition and some people were making and selling moonshine. Neither Bob nor Don ever resorted to making moonshine as some of their neighbors had done. They were getting by with their gardens and fruit trees and along with their cattle they were getting by quite well. Don would even sometimes take food in exchange for repairing someone's automobile. Many times they would share produce with some of their neighbors who were less fortunate. Other times they would trade fruit from their orchard for something others had that they could use. A lot of the time they just gave what they had to others who were in need.

Jean was telling Martha about letters she had received from a friend's daughter. "Different ones back home must be having a hard time making ends meet. Just read what Patricia has written. Kind of makes you wonder."

The friend's daughter wrote:

"**November 3, 1933** Didn't you get my last letter that I wrote? You did not answer it. You did not say what you were doing, you know. I am staying with Ernie Jones' wife here in town, going to school. I have two more years of school left.

Is it possible that you do not know that the Federals caught Ernie and a bunch of others here in town that were making moonshine, and that he is in jail at the county seat. I'll send you the report of it from the paper. He will be out the 1st of February if Letty can rake up enough to pay his fine. If not, he will have to stay until the 6th of March. He has been in jail ever since the 22nd of May. Him and others that were caught. Too bad wasn't it? It seems as though none of us will ever get ahead, or get a break at anything we try.

Work is very scarce here as it seems to be everywhere. Several neighbors are making moonshine and others are selling it for them. Everyone is scared of getting caught. Some feel desperate because there is no work."

"I know of one family that cannot find work and they have no place to live so they have gone out into the woods and made a makeshift shelter from pine tree limbs. The trees give them a little privacy and they have a cook stove in there, so I guess it must help hold the heat in a bit, but it is not weather tight by any means. It isn't much of a shelter and if they are still there later this winter, they will freeze to death. I don't think it is of any help either when it rains. Something needs to be done for the people who are in these kind of troubles."

"There are rumors though that the government is planning on creating work for people to do. I have heard it is to be called the Civilian Conservation Corps, or the C.C. C's for short. Something has to be done and soon. Things can't go on this way too much longer. It seems like there is the possibility that the prohibition will be done away with so then there will not be any market for moonshine any more. Maybe that is a good thing. People should not be so desperate to feed their families that they feel they have to break the law to do so.

"Some of the young men around here are joining the U. S. Army because there is no work for them and some of their families are really desperate. It sure is too bad. It isn't very easy to get into the army either. Another disturbing thing is all the troubles in Europe. I sure hope we never get into any of their troubles after the war that ended so few years ago."

"I must get this in the mail. Bye for now. I thought you would want to know what was going on even if it wasn't very good news."

Love, Patricia

Martha was sad that all this stuff was going on and told her mother "I think we are very fortunate, indeed. While we don't have as much as we used to have in the way of money, we have our health, our loving families, and we do have plenty to eat. Not everyone can say that, can they?"

"There is much rumbling about those problems in Europe that may lead to war. It hasn't been too long since the end of the World War that was to end all wars, and everyone is worried that there may be another one. The banks have closed down and people have no way of getting their money out. The thing that has saved our families is we were not in debt when the stock market crashed and we try to be self-sufficient. I know Don is struggling, but at least no one in our family is going hungry and we all have good shelter".

"There is terrible news of troubles all over the world. The Monarchy in Spain just disintegrated last year, there are problems between Japan and China, all kinds of unrest in Ireland. The whole world seems to be in some kind of a mess. I hope we never get involved in any of their troubles so that we get dragged into it."

A couple of weeks later, Jean heard from Patricia again.

Patricia wrote:

"**Dec. 5, 1933** The Johnson's place was raided a few days ago, but the Federals didn't find anything because the Johnson men found out earlier that there was a possibility that they were next, so they dismantled their still and threw it down the old well some place on the old homestead. Everyone is scared.

When the Smith farm was raided the Federals didn't find anything but they told old man Jake's son that he had better leave the country as they were going to get him sooner or later. He believed them so he packed up his family and headed to some relatives further back East. I think they had cousins who were farmers.

"Enough people have been in jail over this moonshine business that they are getting pretty scared. No one wants to go to jail, and when the men go to jail their families are left to fend for themselves any way they can. Too many people are desperate and something will have to be done soon.

"I think some more of the young boys are joining the CCC's to help their families.

"I have also heard the government is starting something for families with children called ADC—Aid for Dependent Children. All this should help.

Anyway, we all hope this depression will end soon."

Love Patricia

"I sure hope things get better for all these people before too long. Times are very hard for too many people." offered Jean.

"Opportunities for work seemed to be developing with the government building dams on the Columbia River and also on the Colorado River. With the building of those dams the cities would also grow so maybe things will improve soon. We surely hope so."

A few months later Martha told her mother, "I hate to hear that people are still having such a hard time. I know the lines at the food kitchens are long any more. Every once in a while someone will knock on our door and ask if we have some work they can do for a meal. I never turn them away and when they leave I send a little food with them. I wish I could do more for them."

Jean told her daughter she had the same thing happen also. "It is so sad to see the misery some people face. Homeless, lonely, and sometimes often hungry."

"Do you ever feel threatened by these strangers when so many of them come to your door?" asked Jean.

Martha answered, "No one has ever seemed to intimidate me when they came, but there is always the first time. So far everyone just seems to be hungry and down on their luck. With no work available they have run out of resources it seems. So far, everyone who has stopped in has offered to work for their food, and they seem to do it willingly."

It was several months before Jean heard from Patricia again.

Chapter 14

✦

Frank Confides In Martha

THIS REMINDED JEAN about the fellow living in the cabin up the hill from Martha.

She inquired about him "Isn't his name Frank Smithson? I mean the man you bought your place from. Is he still there?"

"Oh yes, he is there some of the time. He met a woman in California when he was spending time down there a while back. They are evidently corresponding quite frequently. Sometimes he lets me read his letters. He may have been serious about her, but he now seems a bit dejected. I hope maybe one of the letters tells why."

Jean noticed the time was getting late in the afternoon so noted "It's time to gather the kids up and go home. They have so much fun playing together they hate to go home.

You were right when you said I would enjoy having

children at my age. It has been such a wonderful blessing that it is so hard to believe. I am also following your example of breast feeding my babies. I am glad you set the example. It sure is a lot easier than having to sterilize bottles all the time or to have to carry bottles around, or having to get up in the middle of the night to heat a bottle. I have a hard time though getting over the way that woman called you a cow."

Martha laughed, "I don't think she meant it the way it sounded, even if it was a bit crude. I have to laugh when I think of it any more."

"It's nice you can laugh about it now. It probably was not very funny at the time.

I guess there was no other supply of milk for that poor unfortunate baby, but to have someone say "**Who cares who milks the cow**" at such a time isn't what most people would think of saying to someone.

Martha laughed again and told her mother. "I really think it's hilarious when I think of it now. It will be something to tell our kids when they get older and can appreciate hearing about such things."

"I must go now, but next time I come, why don't you tell me about Frank. He sounds like he could have some interesting tales to tell if he has been to California." said Jean. "I'd like to hear what he has to say about that part of the country. I would like to go there some day. I want to see how citrus fruit grows on trees and maybe even pick an orange or a grapefruit right off the tree."

Bob and Martha had Frank to dinner at least once a month from the time they moved into their new house whenever he wasn't traveling down to California. He seemed to appreciate it. He evidently was quite lonesome and visiting with Bob and Martha and their family helped him to dispel some of the loneliness he had after the loss of his family. He was always glad to help out whenever he could with the chores, but otherwise kept to his cabin.

The next time Jean visited she asked Martha if she had heard anything more about Frank's trips to California. The conversation led to information about some letters.

Martha informed Jean that Frank had talked to Bob and asked his opinion, and Bob told Frank he would have better results if he talked to Martha and her mother about what was bothering him. Bob had told Frank he had more confidence in the opinion of the two ladies than in anyone else. Consequently he gave a couple of letters to Martha to read and wanted her opinion and advice. He told her it would take all the letters to be able to understand the situation. He would give them to Martha a couple at a time over a period of six months.

One time when Frank had decided to take a trip to California to visit a niece and nephew who had moved there, he must also have decided to work while there. He was evidently in Los Angeles when that big earthquake hit in Long Beach. It must have been a terribly big one. Kind of scary. Some people were so displaced it was hard for relatives to locate them for quite a while afterwards.

After he had come back he seemed to want to share the letters he had received from a young woman while he was there. It was as if he thought of Martha and Bob as if they were his family. He seemed quite dejected and sad and wanted to confide in them. Then by June he had given Bob the six months worth of letters for Martha to read. He also seemed not to care if Martha shared the letters with her mother. He must want their opinions. Evidently he really was not over the loss of his family although it was several years earlier and whatever happened in California had renewed his feelings of loss.

While in California Frank had evidently worked some of the time and looked for more work whenever that job ended. He had to earn enough to pay the property taxes on the land he had purchased after selling the farm to Bob and Martha. He was probably like everyone else, lost by the closing of the banks. Everyone's money was tied up or lost. Only the ones with jobs were mildly affected by the depression and were unaffected by the bank closures, probably because they did not use the bank and simply had cash in their pockets. People moved together to save on expenses or to survive at all. A few people who owned houses that were vacant would let others move into the house so it would not deteriorate and those moving into them would keep the house repaired instead of paying rent. It worked both ways. People showed their appreciation by taking care of anything that needed to be done and no one even thought of vandalizing someone else's property.

"I guess this depression is something affecting everyone in one way or another. I think these letters explain a lot of why Frank is currently depressed. I wish we could help him somehow. I wish he could meet someone here who would interest him. He needs a family of his own. Let's see what the letters are about."

"The lady's name is Jennifer." volunteered Martha. "She wrote to Frank around **January 1st 1933** to tell him how happy she was that he had sent her a beautiful rose that she assumed he had grown in his own yard at the house he lived in there in California. She also mentioned that she had heard he was a good housekeeper."

"We sure have found him to be neat and clean"volunteered Martha. Jennifer also mentioned that she hoped to see him quite soon. She was also happy that he had found a little work and that he could find some more if he wanted it. Maybe times would get a little better soon.

Jennifer mentioned, too, that she wished he would not go stay with his brother on his ranch as he had asked him to do unless it would help him to better himself. She thinks if he went he would make a very fine looking cowboy and that she wished she could be there with him. She was sorry that the job in Long Beach didn't turn out. To quote her words she wrote "Never mind Frank, better days are coming. As you say, maybe our ship will come in some day with lots of good things for us. We can at least live in hopes even though we die in despair. She closed with saying she could enjoy a snowball fight with him if he were there with her even if she caught a severe cold. That it would be worth it.

There evidently was quite a bit of snow where she was living. Then she signed it "as ever, your Jenny."

"Well, Martha, it sounds like she is sweet on him. Do you suppose he's in love with her?"

"He's a lonely man, and I wouldn't be surprised if he was also sweet on her. Only time will tell."

When Martha finished telling about the letter, Jean asked "What happened to the money Frank received for the farm you folks bought from him."

Martha said "I think he sent some to his brother who has the farm, and the rest of it was in the bank when it shut down. All funds in the banks are frozen and nobody has money available. We are all in the same boat.

Fortunately he did buy that piece of property close to ours that has a large stand of timber on it. It should be worth quite a bit some day if he hangs on to it and can pay the taxes in the meantime. That is probably why he has been trying so hard to find work in Los Angeles. The property taxes have to be paid or you can lose the land to the state. Taxes aren't very high on unimproved property, but even a small amount can be hard to pay during these times of high unemployment.

While he lives here in the cabin he has access to our gardens, which he always helps with, plus he hunts for deer or elk for meat, which he always shares with us."

"Frank was so terribly lonesome is probably the reason he wanted us to read the letter. He gave them to Bob when I insisted on knowing why he seemed to be so unhappy. I also believe there is more to it than this though. I'll let you know if he gives me any more information.

It was only two weeks later that another letter had come dated **January 12,1933.** Jennifer wrote thanking Frank again for another beautiful rose. She was fretting that he was not able to find work.She mentioned again something about a Long Beach job that he evidently did not get. Then she changed the subject and told him not to fall for a woman named Marie, or her sister, because if he did she would be jealous. Then she said Ha! Ha! like she meant it as a joke. She described Reno as the smallet large place she ever come across, stating that she would get a stiff neck from rubbernecking at the tall buildings, then mentioned it was plenty cold and that she had a nasty cold that went from better one day to worse the next. She told how she missed everyone. She hasn't said why she is in Reno, but Reno is where a lot of people go to get a divorce. She also mentioned if he got a new car she would like to help him break it in. She said there wasn't any place to go and that everyone went to bed every night at nine or ten. She ended that letter with saying she had kind thoughts of him.

She was trying to be comical about the car, unless he had one he wrecked, but he didn't say anything to us. I think he still has the car he purchased from Don before he left. We only know what was in the letter. I should ask him, but feel he would volunteer the information if he wanted to really talk about it.

Jennifer also must have been trying to be funny, because Reno, Nevada is a very small town and I doubt if there are any real tall buildings there.

"Jennifer had mentioned that he was a good housekeeper. I guess I had noticed that he kept everything quite neat and clean, too. He also keeps the outside of the cabin in good order too, which makes us happy" allowed Martha.

"Frank looked quite sad today and I think he received another letter, which probably explains it. There is more going on than meets the eye. I'll let you know if there is anything more to tell. I feel bad that he is so sad. He really needs a good wife to take care of him. I don't know why, but I don't think things are going any too well with him and this Jennifer. He seems to be holding back for some reason. Of course if she is not free, maybe he has a good reason to hesitate. I guess time will tell."

Chapter 15

An Apology Arrives

A FEW DAYS later Jean asked Martha, "Remember when I came to you and told you I was going to have a baby? You talked to me and it made me think. I am so glad you did, and those two children I had after that talk have been the lights of my life, and that's also true for my husband. You were sure right about that and we are very happy."

"Martha, you really do inspire people to confide in you. That is probably why Frank wanted to talk to you and gave you his letters."

"Oh, and Martha, you and I are so lucky, the men we married are wonderful, kind men, and I am so proud of both of them."

Martha responded with great enthusiasm "You are so very, very right. We both married well. It was a great blessing that I got a wonderful son and that I married his father. I thank God every day for my good fortune. Bob is a wonderful man and I dearly love him. His son has become my son in every sense of the word. I love them both very dearly. Our meeting was not very conventional, but it has turned out well for all of us. I could not have done any better."

Jean suddenly remarked to Martha, "I almost forgot to tell you that Rosalyn wrote a letter to me and apologized for stealing your letters. She admitted she was wrong to be jealous of you and asked us to forgive her. Now, she also wants to know if she can come to see us here. She wants to apologize in person. I am inclined to let her come."

"It might be hard to forgive her, Mother. It was a terrible thing for her to do. Jealousy, though, can cause people do some awful things. It is something I would have to think about, but it is up to you. It must be hard for her to apologize and she would really have to be sorry for her actions to volunteer to come all this way to do so."

"Martha, it has been a long time now since she stole those letters, in fact it has been several years, and evidently it has been bothering her conscience all these years. I am inclined to forgive her now. At least if she comes to visit it can heal all our hearts about what she did. I think she has been a very unhappy person and probably needs forgiveness from us?"

"All right, Mother. If she comes we can listen to her excuses and then we can all go on from there and maybe never mention it again. Let me know when she is due to arrive. Maybe we can arrange for a family get-together first, and then some kind of a get-together party for the neighborhood if she is here for any length of time. Everyone looks forward to any kind of gathering we can plan."

"Oh, and Mother, Frank telephoned from Don's shop and will pick the kids up from school this afternoon. He had his car at Don's Repair Shop for some kind of repairs. He will be driving his car past the school so offered to do so. Let me know if and when Rosalyn comes, will you please." added Martha.

It did not take Rosalyn long to decide to visit Martha and Jean once she heard from Jean that she would be welcome. She took a leave of absence from her school teaching job, and she had the summer off.

Rosalyn was a woman who had never been married. Word had evidently not gotten around about her theft of letters written by Martha to her family as this would have seriously alienated her from most of her acquaintances and she would have been avoided. As a teacher, she would also have lost her job and maybe never been able to get a teaching job again. Teachers are required to be of good character. Rosalyn herself had drawn into a shell and avoided contacting people. This was not good. It seems she had decided to turn over a new leaf in her life when she contacted Jean and Martha and apologized for what she had done. She just had to apologize in person in addition to the one by letter. It was a wonder that her letter theft information had not become public. Teachers had to have a perfect record in order to teach. The female teachers could not even have a gentleman friend. It was in their contracts. Teachers had to be beyond reproach in every way.

Evidently only the family knew about her stealing the letters as the school board would have promptly fired her if they had even had a rumor of such a thing.

It was a month later when Rosalyn arrived in Mesa

Ridge. She was a woman about thirty years of age, not real slim, but neither could she be considered fat by any means. She was of medium build and probably about 5 feet 2 inches in height. Her hair was a light brown color and she wore it shoulder length. She was not what could be called a real beauty, but she was quite attractive.

Jean and her husband, John, met Rosalyn at the stage depot. The bus was about ½ an hour late. After the long ride they decided she was probably quite tired so Jean suggested the first thing they should do was take her to their farm first and let her rest and get settled after having some lunch. Visiting with other family members could wait until the next day. The next day was Saturday, which would work out just right for the family to meet each other and they would all go to Martha's and Bob's place for the afternoon and have a big picnic by the creek.

After all the greetings and first talk settled down, Rosalyn was awed at the beauty of the place as it had been made into by Bob and Martha. It was like a beautiful park with the small creek and the improvements made by Bob. who had built a picnic table with benches. He had put a little bridge over the creek that reminded her of pictures of Japanese gardens. There was a set of swings for the children and he had put up a large round stock tank to use like a swimming pool for the children, and he had fixed it so it could be drained in the winter so it would not be ruined by ice that would form during freezing weather. Further down, the creek was deep enough for adults to swim if they wanted to. The children were not allowed near the water, though, unless there was an adult with them, as there was always the possibility of drowning. As a precaution, Bob had put up a fence around the water areas as well as a play area that was fenced separately so the children could play safely.

Just before they were to eat lunch, Frank arrived to join the family. He had been invited but had been unable to come earlier. Rosalyn and Frank were introduced and they all sat down to eat.

Rosalyn noted that Frank was an attractive man of about 40 years of age. He had slightly curly hair that was still red, but was beginning to turn a little grey. She was surprised to hear that he had once owned this farm, and this is when she learned he sold it because it brought back too many memories from losing his family. Still it was strange that he lived in a cabin on the property anyway. It was then he explained that it was the house that reminded him of the family in such a way that he felt he could not put up with the hurt. Every room in the house would remind him of the loss of his wife and children. He then told her he had purchased another nearby piece of property that maybe one day he would develop into another place. This other place had timber on it that could be made into lumber to build a house. There was also a creek running through the property, just like this one and which had a beautiful spot where a nice home could be built some day. Now that telephones and electrical lines were in the area it would be feasible to build now. He had a location in mind of where he wanted to build a house that would be very nice. "Would you like to see it some day?" Frank asked her. He was always willing to show it to anyone who was interested.

"I'd love to see it" was Rosalyn's reply. She didn't think anything of it at the time. To her it was just a polite answer.

They had all been talking and eating for quite a while when John spoke up and said, "I almost forgot, there is a party and dance at the community center two weeks from today and we are all invited."

These get-togethers were always welcome and everyone looked forward to attending. The only thing it ever cost was food which came in the form of pot-luck and it was always generous and good. Anyone who played an instrument would bring it and they would take turns playing them so no one ever missed out in having fun. In these hard times everyone took advantage of free entertainment and really had a good time of it.

Frank was quick enough to realize if he wanted a companion for this dance he had to act quickly so he asked Rosalyn right then and there if she would accompany him to the dance on that evening. She was happy to say "Yes."

When the others had gone, Rosalyn asked Martha and Jean about Frank. Could they tell her anything about him. That was when Martha mentioned that he was a very reliable man, but he probably had a girlfriend in California, but he was not engaged to her that they knew of. Rosalyn told them he had invited her to accompany him to the dance and she had agreed to go with him, and was looking forward to it, but did not want to interfere if he had a regular girlfriend. They figured if he was committed to the girl in California that he would not have asked Rosalyn to the dance so she needn't worry, but should go and enjoy herself.

When Martha and Jean were alone, Martha told Jean that she had seen a letter dated **January 21, 1933** from Jennifer stating that she had been quite sick. If it hadn't been for a friend she might have died of pneumonia. Seems the friend came to see her and realizing she was very ill had bundled her up and taken her from Reno to Fallon, Nevada. The friend decided Jennifer needed someone to take care of her and now she had been moved from Reno to Fallon, Nevada. She was better but still weak and shaky.

She claims she misses Frank and that she was now among strangers. The lady she had stayed with in Reno evidently didn't want to or didn't feel obligated to take care of Jennifer when she was so sick and it may have saved her life when the friend moved her from Reno to Fallon. The former lady had evidently felt just calling the doctor was all she needed to do. There had been a very big snow storm, but it didn't seem very cold, and that she hadn't been out of the house. since she arrived in Fallon.

"There was one sentence in that letter that I wonder about. She said "Frank, don't keep me in suspense in regards to that question you want to ask. I assure you I am very much interested." Was that question possibly a proposal. Maybe that is why Frank was so sad looking, but why be sad if it was a proposal. I'm wondering. about that question.

When she closed the letter she said she was very tired. I'm sure she probably was tired if she had had pneumonia. She really must have been very sick if she was confined to the house and couldn't get out."

Jean, there were letters from **January 26th** stating there had been very heavy snow storms and intense cold. The roads were closed and she still hadn't been outside. She was feeling better, but she made reference to that mysterious question she referred to before. Her statement was "I am hapy to kow you feel as you say you do as the feeling is mutual. I only wish you would have spoken before I undertook this trip, because I am under an obligation which is going to be rather hard for me to meet. Kind of a strange statement isn't it? She went on to mention again about the "Long Beach proposition." which must be some kind of a job. Then she asked if he had been to a dance since she had been gone, that it was hard for her to be still but she would be unable to go anyway while sick. Then she said she wished "things were a little bit different with us both and that one day our ship may sail in." She said she didn't mind the snow if she could only go out and enjoy it.

"Jennifer must have been really sick. Sounds to me like she might have had pneumonia" said Jean and Martha in unison. "I think the weather gets pretty cold there in Nevada during the winter months. It sure sounds to me like it does. This lady needs to take care of herself'. They both noted also that she mentions again about their mutual feelings. This could only mean feelings of the heart in my opinion."

"That place where this Jennifer is living sure is cold. She doesn't say why she is there except someone took her to Fallon from Reno because she got very sick" Martha commented. She evidently was so very sick she needed to have someone take care of her." She sent Frank a Valentine, stated that the temperature was 15 below zero. Now that is very cold. It makes me shiver to even think of being that cold. It can get pretty cold here in the winter but I don't think it has ever been that cold since I've lived here."

Jean then asked Martha if she had ever been to Fallon.

Martha answered Jean, "No, I've never bad a chance to go anywhere except around this area, but maybe Bob has been there."

"It sure sounds like the climate is not mild", exclaimed Jean.

"She keeps the mailman pretty busy, I'd say. There are rumors that postge is going to go up to three cents soon. Maybe she is trying to get her letters in before it costs more to mail a letter. Prices keep going up for everything."

"You know, in her next letter on **February 21ˢᵗ** she says she is quite well again. She mentions that for a little while she was going to be free but had to change her mind. Strange isn't it. She also states again that she still feels the way he does, but had he spoken sooner things might have been different. She also gives the opinion that any girl that gets him would be mighty lucky. The weather had become a little warmer, and the snow was melting, and the radio was putting out a lot of static. She must have had the radio on while writing her letters.

"It sounds as if she is over her illness now. It also sounds like something is wrong here. She mentions she thought she would be free by now. Free from what?" commented Jean.

"She mentions about Frank having a hangover, but I have never known him to be a drinking man. Maybe it was just a case of a one time drinking bout that he had too much and it hit him suddenly and pretty hard. It could have been an offbeat suggestion even that he felt like he had a hangover, instead of it being a fact. I guess it could happen to anyone who is not a heavy drinker. I hope it was not because he was unhappy with his relationship with Jennifer. That doesn't sound like the Frank we know."

Jennifer wrote another letter on **March 6, 1933** and started right off asking Frank to understand what she meant by being obligated because she had given her word elsewhere not knowing how Frank felt about her. She also says some party may break off with her, that there is all indications of that and she is hoping for the best. She hoped he would not go away before she came back, that maybe she would be able to say "Well, Frank, I want to go with you." and asked him to understand. She then went on to say they were having lovely weather for a change and she was sorry about his job.

"Did Frank propose to her and she had already promised someone else? It is beginning to sound that way"asked Jean. Also, it sounds a bit like she is stringing him along. I think Frank is a very lonely man. He would make some nice woman a good husband. The loss of his wife and children may be making him hesitate though. In one letter Jennifer refers to someone coming to see her, but wonders if he has plans to fight her in court.This person was in a car accident before he arrived. Evidently the man was not killed, but she makes no further reference to him. Maybe he was the husband she was divorcing. Kind of mysterious isn't it?"

Times had turned pretty hard. All the government places such as the post office, court house, and banks were closed down. This closing down was going on all over the country, not just in one place, but everywhere. The whole country was affected in one way or another, and it affected everyone all over the world and in every state. Some people were trying to sell apples or pencils on the street trying to make a dime so they could buy something they needed. There was no welfare set-ups until the government finally stepped in with some help.

Jennifer had written that she had a relapse. No one could cash a check with the banks closed and everyone was afraid of checks anyway as they don't know if the banks will ever open again. People didn't even have the money to go to a movie. It was still cold in March in Nevada.and elsewhere.

Martha commented to Jean "Besides the cold making her sick, she writes again of banks closing, which must be all over the country as well as right here." She also mentions about an earthquake. I remember reading about a really big one that happened in Long Beach or some place near there" Jean informed Martha. "I am glad something like that isn't happening here I think I would be frightened to death, wouldn't you, Mother?" Martha asked Jean.

Jennifer had written that she had told the lady she lives with what Frank had said about having flowers and earthquakes 12 months out of the year and she sure did get a kick out of that. She said you're not the only one's who have them, they do have them here, and rather often. Now they had snow, rain, and hail this day. But she pointed out that they didn't have freezing weather in the spring They might not have sunshine but there is plenty of moonshine if one knows where to go and money to buy it with.

Martha told of Jennifer's grandmother who is 90 years old. She has lived in Long Beach for a number of years and she cannot seem to find out if she is all right or not. She has tried everything she could think of to locate her but no luck. It is terrible to worry about someone under that knd of circumstance. You don't know if they are alive or if they succumbed to the trauma of the earthquake in Long Beach.

She mentioned a trial or something earlier, so it must have been about a divorce that she mentions here, and she isn't free." She mentions earthquakes again. Sounds like there was more than one." She is still worried about her grandmother. I hope she finds out soon. It's always a big worry to have an elderly relative missing like that.

"Well, prohibition is finally over. Now we can finally have all the beer, cheese, and crackers we can buy, and be within the law to top it off. I still think it was more fun drinking bootleg," wrote Jennifer.

"She has mentioned her grandmother again. She still hasn't heard from her. That can be an awful worry. Evidently that earthquake in Long Beach was a really big one. I'm glad we don't get them here" Martha remarked.

Jean replied, "Don"t be too sure that we won't get one here. Earthquakes may be more common in California, but they can happen any place in the world. We may just be fortunate that they arre not common here at all.

"I guess we probably are very fortunate at that," replied Martha. The end of prohibition has undoubtedly put the moonshine business out of a job. Probably it's for the best in the long run. There have been some pretty bad things happening in the eastern part of the United States because of the sale of moonshine. It had caused some fights that ended in death where gangs fought each other over territory. This should end that part of the gangster era." Jean brought out. "I sure hope some other kind of evil does not take its place."

"I sure hope not, also. It got pretty nasty at times."

Jennifer wrote that she was leaving for home on

June 2nd and should arrive home on the 3rd of June. She mentioned something not ending until the end of May, which must be referring to a divorce being final. Now I wonder what has happened to her grandmothr. She may have been badly injured in that terrible earthquake they had in Long Beach. She might have a very good reason to worry, but I sure hope not. She also mentions that she would not nor could not be home before June 3rd. Here is Jennifer's final letter to Frank.

June 10, 1933. Dear Frank, Received your letter, was very happy to hear from you. Am very glad to know your sister is so much better. Frank, I sure wish you were here, as I am going to be married June 18th. Would love to have you at my wedding, but no such luck. Ma and Dad Carter sure were glad to have me back home, but say they are sorry to have to lose me again, just when they got me back. Anyhow, Frank, wish me luck, as I no doubt will need it.

We are having a church wedding, then a dinner afterwards. If you could possibly join us, your presence would be very welcome to all concerned. Mrs. Carter said for you to write. They moved into the rear house of where they used to live. They too were glad to know you got home safe.

Would have written sooner but have been terribly busy since coming. I arrived home last Sunday night on the 10:25 train. I sure did enjoy the trip. I felt fine and hope to continue to do same. Ma and Dad Carter send their best regards. As ever Jennifer.

"If Frank had been planning on marrying Jennifer,

this letter must have been very devastating to him. She even invites him to her wedding. No wonder Frank has been feeling so down. I don't think Frank has any plans to go back to California any time soon."

"I thought from the earlier letters that this Jennifer was making plans with Frank, but she did say once that he asked her too late, that she had already made a promise to someone else," remarked Martha. "Too bad if it broke his heart. I hate to hear of that as Frank is a very nice person. I hope he finds someone up closer to here. When he lost his whole family a few years back he really never seemed to fully recover."

"It surely would be hard to lose a whole family and in such a tragic way as a fire. I know it would take me a long time to get over something like that. I guess life has to go on though, in spite of terrible things happening to our loved ones.

"Jean asked Martha "Why did Frank give you such personal letters to read!"

Martha replied, "I am not quite sure, but I had insisted on knowing why he seemed to be so unhappy, and he confided to me that talking to me was like talking to his sister and getting her advice, and her mending his wounds"

Jean replied, "Martha, you do affect people that way. You listen, which a lot of people do not do. Sometimes that is all it takes to help some get their heads on straight. Maybe all he needs is for someone to listen to him and the letters are saying part of what he needs to talk about. I will bet he will be telling you more in person one of these days.

Actually, I noticed that Frank was almost like an uncle

to your children. They seem to like him also. Sometimes a good friend is more valuable than gold.

"Oh, maybe he will tell me more some day. Mother, Frank will pick the kids up from school this afternoon. He had his car at Don's Repair Shop for some kind of repairs He will be driving his car past the school so offered to do so. He offers to do this whenever he goes into town. It helps a lot."

"Is this the car he took to California?" aked Jean.

"Oh, yes it is. He bought it from Don before he left the last time."

"We bought ours a short time before Frank bought his. Of course Don was nice enough to give our families a big discount, but $750 for a car is sure an expensive way to spend money when wages are only a dollar a day, but we needed it." explained Jean.

"How about the cost of gasoline?" returned Martha. "Frank said he had to pay 15 cents a gallon when he was in the mountains on the way home. I suppose it costs more to deliver gas when a station is high up in the mountains. The price was 11 cents a gallon everywhere else, the same as here at home."

"I sure hope the price never gets any higher. It gets pretty hard to pay such prices. If the prices keep going up I suppose the next thing you know everything else will be going higher too I hope it's wages and not other costs of living, don't you?"

"Say, Martha, do you still ride that big black horse you had a while back? I never seem to see him around any more.?"

"Oh yes, I ride him every once in a while, but I don't have the time I used to have to spend. We have him out in a far pasture. He still objects to anyone else riding him, so he doesn't get used too much any more. He just seems to be a one person animal. Most people just remember his old reputation as being a mean horse, and are afraid of him. I think they don't need to be, but I don't encourage anyone to test him as things are working out all right the way they are. He seems to be the kind of animal that you have to make friends with him before he makes friends with you. That is all I did to get his cooperation and no one else has made the effort since. He isn't mean, he's just not one to come forward on his own to become your friend."

"You have a nice bunch of horses. You have the reputation of being good with them, don't you?"

"Well, I do like them. Grandpa taught me quite a bit about horses when I was younger. Remember how he used to take me with him. I always enjoyed our times together, and he taught me all I know about them, which has come in mighty handy since we have this nice place to raise them. I enjoy the animals which makes it so much better to take care of them. It doesn't become a chore that way. It also helps with our income."

"I must get busy, I'm having Frank and Rosalyn over for supper tonight. Why don't you and your family come also. It makes a nice group for our families to get together."

"See you at six."

Chapter 16

✦

Frank And Rosalyn Get Acquainted

Jean and Martha saw that Rosalyn had really been sorry for her past actions and they were enjoying her visit. They also noted something else. Rosalyn was like another person than she had been. She was happy and seemed to be having a great deal of fun. Frank was calling on her and they were exploring the country, sightseeing, and the amazing thing was that she was seeming to like the country. Rosalyn had always been a city girl. They hadn't believed she would be attracted to the kind of rural life they were living, but she sure appeared to be enthralled with everything.

One day Rosalyn remarked to Martha, "Frank told me he had been in love with a girl named Jennifer while he was in Californis, but she ended up marrying somebody else in the end. He had been heartbroken. He also said he had confided in you about her letters and that you had listened to him, and he now realized it was probably a good thing that they didn't get married under the circumstances."

Martha then told Rosalyn, "All I did was read the letters, but that did seem to make him feel better for some reason. I had asked him why he was so down-hearted and he handed me the letters. He wants me to let you read the last one. Her goodbye to him."

Martha continued, "I think he was so downhearted because he had lost his first family and losing out with this girl was adding too much to his first grief."

"Is he really over her,?" asked Rosalyn.

"It may be too early to tell, honey, but if you are interested in him and he is interested in you, a little time will tell. Just read that last letter, then you'll know."

"I am very interested in him, but I don't want him on the rebound as it might not last if it is. I learned my lesson with you,. I am still paying for that mistake. I sure did not know that Jackson was such an abuser, and it is a good thing I did not get him, and I am sorry things turned out the way that they did for you with him. I guess I did not have enough wealth to make him interested in me. I am truly sorry it was so bad for you."

"Rosalyn, please forget it I think you suffered as much as I did the way things turned out. In the long run, everything is now all right."

"Time will tell if broken hearts are mended. Sometimes a healed heart is much stronger than it was before it got broken. If you find you love Frank, I think you could be happy with him and I doubt he could do any better than having you. Just take your time and things will work out in the end."

"Thanks, Martha., I really appreciate what you are telling me. You are so fortunate that you have Bob. He is a wonderful person and I am so happy for you. That little boy of yours sure is a jewel as well." "All of the children are growing up so fast."

"Yes, I was very fortunate the way things turned out. I have a beautiful family, I love my home, and I do hope everything goes well for you too." Martha replied.

All went well for the next two weeks. Frank and Rosalyn were seeing a lot of each other and everyone was looking forward to the coming barn dance.

A few days after the barn dance Don and Annabelle had the bad news happen just as they thought everything was looking up. The younger boy, Michael, came down with a serious sickness that might possibly be polio. There were a great many cases coming down all around the country. It was a devastating worry everywhere.

Now everyone was frightened that more of the children might get it also. He was very sick. They were frightened for his life and although he did not die, he was left with crippled legs and had to have rehabilitation treatments. He was going to need constant exercise. They would need help as it was more than one person could handle. Rosalyn decided she was free and she could help, so she moved into their home so she would not need to travel, which would save time also. Every day she would take turns with Annabelle in masaging his legs and exercising them. Rosalyn was also a teacher so he did not lose out on his schooling.

Yes, Rosalyn was making up for her mistaken actions and jealousy from before. She was also becoming quite dearly loved by the family.

They never found out for sure what kind of illness Michael had, but also none of the other children came down sick. Fortunately it turned out that it was not Polio. His legs became strong again with Rosalyn's help. Michael would always have a limp, but otherwise he appeared to have no other problems with his legs.

All of the children took their turns at chicken pox, measles, and mumps as well as any of the other diseases common to children. It seems that any time one child comes down with an illness, all the rest also end up with the same illness. This seems to be the way epidemics start and of course school is the gathering place. It starts out with one child being slightly sick but the illness is not recognized and when it is it is too late, so life goes on like that. These illnesses made the rounds of all the children in the family for several weeks so he did not get behind the other children in his schooling.

Rosalyn was offered the job of teaching the Mesa Ridge school for the next school year and decided to take it. The pay was to be twenty dollars a month. She signed for a years contract. She also decided she liked it there and had another cousin pack up her belongings and ship them to her. She was moving permanently to Mesa Ridge. In the meantime, Frank Smithson was escorting her to all the local get-togethers. Other gentlemen were also taking notice of her, but she really liked Frank so she did not encourage anyone else very strongly, although she also did not completely turn them away as she was not committed to Frank as of yet.

With all the family nearby, Rosalyn was quite happy. She was enjoying her teaching job, and was glad to have the job considering the hard times. The usual pay of twenty dollars a month for a teacher was what she was used to so she was satisfied.

The unrest in Europe was heating up and it was looking more and more like war there. The United States seemed to be staying out of it pretty well as long as nothing happened to drag the United States into it. In November of 1933 the United States had recognized the Soviet Union as the government of Russia. On March 4, 1933 Franklin Delano Roosevelt was inaugurated as President of the United States. Sometime in 1933 Hitler had been given dictatorial powers for four years, but he continued on longer. The unrest in Europe was continuing.

Frank seemed to be paying more and more attention to Rosalyn, but it seemed he was a bit hesitant about a marriage proposal. It was Martha who came right out one day and boldly asked him what his intentions toward Rosalyn were. He backed away from her for a bit and than said, "I'm afraid to ask her. I'm afraid she will turn me down."

"OK Frank! How do you know she will turn you down if you don't ask her?"

Martha scolded him.

"Well, I guess you are right." he replied.

Martha then reminded Frank of an earlier letter he had received, "I think I remember you gave me a letter a few months ago stating a girl named Jennifer was interested in the same thing you were interested in, which was a question not asked by you. You evidently waited too long and she gave her word to someone else. Are you going to do the same thing again? I think there are others who could be interested in Rosalyn if you are not. Don't keep her hanging if you are not interested in marriage. I know she likes you so very much, so please get with it or release her."

"You are over Jennifer aren't you? You aren't yearning for her any longer are you?" Martha continued. "I think Rosalyn would make you a good wife, but if you have no marriage intentions you need to let her go. It is the only responsible thing to do, because I know she really does love you."

A few days later, Rosalyn asked Martha and Bob if she could have the family gather together at their place and she would furnish a cake and sandwiches for the occasion. "I think it would be nice for all of us and I don't have room at my place. I sure would appreciate it if you wouldn't mind."

"Of course I don't mind, honey. We always love to have family get-togethers."

Chapter 17

✦

The Announcement

ROSALYN BROUGHT PLENTY of sandwiches and lemonade. She did not bring the cake in for a while. They thought she had probably left it in Frank's car for some reason. They served the sandwiches and then about the time they finished eating the sandwiches a delivery truck drove up and a woman was coming up to the door with a package, and another person with another package was following. How strange. All together there were three packages. The kids were especially excited. It looked like someone was bringing presents or something.

Martha answered the door and the delivery people came in with their packages and put them on the table. Everyone was curious, of course. These people started to open all the packages.How strange. Most people opened their own packages. The first package they opened contained dishes and decorations, the second one was ice cream. At that the children became really excited. There were plenty of expectant and curious children around. Finally came the third package and as it was opened the caterers called out "SURPRISE." and inside was a beautiful cake decorated with roses, and in the center was a bell beside the names—"**FRANK AND ROSALYN**." This was their special announcement that they were engaged. Of course congratulations were in order.

Then the caterers started to chant a little ditty, to everyone's delight:

Frank and Rosalyn as you can see
Want you to know they are happy as can be
They plan to marry as soon as their house can be built
It may take a while cause it's like a quilt
They have to put it together piece by piece
They invite friends, relatives and nephew and niece.
Do come to the wedding, you are all invited
The coming event has us really excited.

They announced that they would be married as soon as their new house could be built on the property Frank had purchased a few years before, right after he sold the house that Bob and Martha had bought from him. There was a spot on the property that he had shown Rosalyn one day, and that is where the house was to be built.

During the afternoon Rosalyn again told Martha and Jean she still felt remorse at what she had done and felt she hardly deserved ending up so happy, and thanked them for being so kind to her. She would always be grateful that they had forgiven her even if she didn't deserve it. The two women told her it was time she quit punishing herself, she had redeemed herself, and it was time for all of them to forget what had happened.

While the house was being built they would help Rosalyn make plans for her wedding. and time would go so fast that the day would be upon them before they knew it.

Chapter 18

✦

Don't Mess Up My Kids Yard

IN THE MEANTIME life was going smoothly for everyone, until one day when a neighbor informed Frank that they had seen a lot of cattle grazing on his property and they figured he was starting to raise cattle. Frank immediately investigated and found that someone was not only illegally using his property without permission, but they had cut his fences in order to do so. As if that wasn't enough, someone was stealing some of his building supplies. When Frank confronted the culprits, they denied their actions, and they didn't know anything whatsoever about any stolen building supplies. Then Frank told them it was odd that the cattle knew how to cut fences and to saw down the trees used as barriers across the road in order to get through to the pastures. They threatened Frank that he could not stop them. In turn the thieves were informed they would find that their cattle would end up in his cupboard and on his table if they were found on his property again. Frank was very forceful and they must have believed him, as the cattle were removed.

About the same time that Frank had trouble with someone's cattle Bob was having some of the same kind of trouble and the ones inside his property managed to get up near his house and had left cow pies where the children could get into them. This is the one time when Martha saw Bob lose his temper. Why should his children have to watch out for cow manure when they were playing? These thieves told both Bob and Frank that their property wasn't being used for anything important and they had a right to run cattle on the unused forest land if they wanted to. Bob asked them why they thought the forest land wasn't being used. They didn't have a satisfactory answer. Bob used some very strong language and the thieves backed away. Bob also told them he would consider their cattle was a gift to him and he was going to butcher any that were on his property the next day. He also informed them he was being generous in giving them until the next day to get them out of there.

Someone had called the sheriff and he drove up about the time Bob finished telling the thieves he would butcher their cattle. The sheriff heard enough of the conversation that he spoke up and said if Bob or Frank butchered any of the cattle he would not object so they had better get out and right immediately. They left and the cattle were not in sight the next day. The sheriff told both Frank and Bob that these cattle men probably would steal someone's cattle if they had a chance and that they should keep an eye on them in case they tried something again. After all, these fellows could use the National Forest land to graze their cattle if they weren't too lazy to drive them a little farther and to obtain a permit so it would be legal. The sheriff also said he doubted that these were the same ones stealing Frank's building materials as they probably would not have a use for what was missing so far. Frank would have to secure his property a little better. While people usually did not go around taking material from someone building a house, things were beginning to tempt some where it never used to be a temptation. Lock it up now.

The sheriff informed both Bob and Frank he thought the men driving the cattle were not the owners themselves but probably only worked for the owner, and doubted if the cattleman knew his employees were acting in the way they did. He would try to contact the cattleman himself and see if he wouldn't straighten the employees out as to where they took his cattle. Of course, they hoped he would cooperate with them too.

Rosalyn picked the children up after school one Friday evening and when she got them home, she offered to take them to a movie the next day if Martha did not object. She would also include Don's family if Don and Annabelle agreed.

The children had their choice: Did they want to see Bill Boyd who played Hop-a-long Cassidy or Gene Autry, or Tex Ritter, or was it Roy Rogers they wanted to see? Of course it was all of them. When they could not agree as to which one they wanted to see on Saturday, Rosalyn spoke up and told them she would see to it that maybe if they were real good she would take them to see all of them, but not all in the same day. It would have to be one each week. One time they even got to see Smiley Burnette in person. Another time Roy Rogers appeared in person.

All of this was so exciting and they looked forward to go to the movies.

They might have the good fortune of the movie theater showing a double feature so they could see two movies all on the same day. There was also Buck Jones, Bob Steele, Ken Maynard, and a few others if things worked out. Occasionally there would be an old movie with Tom Mix too. They were all one bunch of happy kids. Now they were all going to be cowboys when they grew up. Of course some of those movies with Gene Autry were going to be serial shows so they would only see one section a week. This made a good excuse to go to the movies every week. Any of the kids still under 12 years of age got in for ten cents so they had to save up their allowances if they wanted to go every week.

One day they heard one of the boys singing a song they had heard the cowboys sing in their movie. They thought it was Ken Maynard who sang the song, but they were not too sure. It went something like:

I'm Captain Jinks of the Horse Marines
I feed my horse on corn and beans
And court young ladies in their teens
For I'm the pride of the Army.
I teach young ladies how to dance
How to dance, how to dance.
I teach young ladies how to dance
For I'm the pride of the Army.

Then they started repeating the song over. The kids must have enjoyed the movie. Now they were cowboys who could sing too.

Of course, Rosalyn was seeing the kids enjoy themselves and after all she was still a kid herself so she was sure to enjoy it too.

Chapter 19

✦

Visitors Coming

ROSALYN VISITED WITH Martha and Jean after returning from taking the children to the movies and informed them she might soon be getting a visit from a friend she knew in college. The friend would also be bringing her mother, who lived in New York. The friend, Geraldine, said her mother wanted to know if it was safe to come to Mesa Ridge with the danger from the Indians. Also would the cowboys be shooting people in front of them? Did they need to be afraid, or would they have protection? Would the rustlers be stealing cattle and put them in danger. How could anyone feel safe in such dangerous country? Do they still use covered wagons? Geraldine's mother was evidently a bit skeptical about the trip and her safety, but wanted to experience the adventure. Would Rosalyn treat her mother accordingly and make the trip exciting for her? She evidently knew her mother's ideas about the far

Western United States. Rosalyn's grandparents had been early settlers in the Dakota territory before it became a state and evidently had told some wild tales to her mother along with her ideas she had formed from the movies.

They all laughed when Rosalyn told them about the letter. Evidently some of the people back there based their ideas on what they saw in the movies and not on anything that was reality. They don't stop to think that the movies are only stories of fictional characters and nothing was very real about them. Hollywood takes liberty with stories.

Geraldine herself knew the truth but it was her mother who thought the western part of the United States was still unsettled and was "Wild and Dangerous" and worried if they *would be safe in coming.

"Let's all meet them in a buckboard when they arrive." exclaimed Jean. "We might as well give them a thrill. Why spoil it with a car."

"They won't see that we now use automobiles until we get them to our home." volunteered Martha. "We can take them the long way home. Let's take the loop road around Mika Peak That road circles through a variety of farms and scenery."

They will think we live miles and miles from town, but will eventually learn the truth, and hopefully will forgive us for the deception. Also, eventually they will find out our little town of Mesa Ridge isn't really far from the bigger city, but it is a small farm community and convenient for those of us who live here." exclaimed Jean.

Rosalyn said "We can go by way of the mountains past some of the gold and silver mines. Then if we go near the forest and the sawmills we will have gone past so many things that maybe they will get straightened out in their minds the reality of things as they really are and we won't embarrass them."

"They will see the Indians on the streets, and will find that they won't look any different from the rest of us either. The only Indians we see in costume are at special events where they deliberately dress that way for show. The very old Indians may dress slightly different, but otherwise they are just like the rest of us." said Jean.

"We can also probably see wild horses and even a few wild burros on that loop road. Sometimes they come grazing close to the highway. I hope they are not too tired from the trip here to enjoy the time it will take to drive around the loop" enjoined Jean.

"I will enjoy that trip also," said Rosalyn.

"We will send Geraldine's mother home with the knowledge of the real way things are in the western part of the United States." added Jean.

There is also a Rodeo scheduled during the time they are here and I'll bet they would enjoy that too" added Rosalyn.

"This ought to be fun" they all agreed.

"While they are here, let's also visit one of the hot springs. They should enjoy soaking in one of them. You can also bring them over to our place to go swimming, but the water will be cold. If the day is hot, the cold would probably be welcome." invited Martha.

"I'll bet they will want to know all about how the water at the hot springs is heated when it comes from out of the ground and not heated in a tank of some kind" remarked Rosalyn.

"While Mother and I do not know these two ladies, I

am sure we will enjoy meeting them and look forward to it. Do plan on entertaining them at our place while they are here. We have lots of room both indoors and out and you are welcome at any time," reiterated Martha.

"Too bad the timing is off for them to attend Franks and my wedding, but they will get to meet him and see what has been done so far on the house we are building." volunteered Rosalyn. "Geraldine has to get back to work. She could not get time off at any other time than now. I am just glad she can come at all."

Rosalyn continued, "Martha, your letting us have the wedding at your place is so nice. Your lovely setting by the creek will be so ideal. I think several of Frank's relatives and friends will be coming up from California too. By that time our house will be done,, but although the house is finished, the yard and surrounding area won't be ready."

"I don't know yet how many will be coming from back home. Although I refer to 'back home' I mean where I used to live. I really am not a city girl any more. I really love it here, and I feel very much at home in this country setting. I am so glad you let me come in spite of what I did. I thank you."

Jean scolded her, "I told you to forget it, didn't I? No permanent harm was done and you have punished yourself much more than any of us could have done. You have made up in full for your error and do not bring it up again. All I ask is that you do not let jealousy get in your way ever again."

Martha also told Rosalyn, "There is a possibility that an old girl friend of Frank's may also be up to the wedding, but she is now married to someone else. I am very sure that Frank is fully over her and you have nothing to worry about as far as she is concerned. Frank loves you dearly. If you start to feel any jealousy about the woman named Jennifer, just come to me and I can assure you that everything is all right and you can relax. You may even find she may become a good friend to you. Old flames usually die out and are not ever revived."

"Thank you Martha, I think I have thoroughly learned my lesson. I love both you and Jean, and you have been so good to me. I have every confidence in Frank and I love him more than I ever dreamed I would love anyone," answered Rosalyn "In fact, Frank told me about Jennifer and also said we would be going to Los Angeles some day and would probably see her. I believe him as he was very sincere about his former feelings concerning Jennifer. She is in his past and the only thing about the future is she is a friend among many friends. I do not feel threatened about Jennifer, thanks to both of you."

Jean and Martha both felt that Rosalyn now realized that jealousy was not worth all the grief it can cause everyone who suffers from it, and that Rosalyn had it under control and it would not ever raise its ugly head again.

"Maybe later we will be able to find out about Jennifer's grandmother and the big earthquake she was in. The last I heard, she had not heard from her grandmother and had not been able to locate her after that terrible big earth shaking deal in Long Beach. I never thought to ask Frank if he ever heard, although I don't think he has heard anything more from California in several months. It must have been quite a frightening event from all I have heard about it. Long Beach really got a big jolt that did a lot of damage, and scared everyone who was in it. I know I would have been very scared." remarked Martha.

The others agreed with Martha. An earthquake must be frightening, although some in California say the small ones don't bother them. They do agree though that they always worry that one like the Long Beach quake will happen again and it does scare everyone. They worry that some day will bring more large quakes that will do so much damage, and especially if it should hit in a large populated area, as that is where the damage is bound to do some harm to both property and to people.

They noted also that Los Angeles is growing into an extremely large city. With it's moderate climate people would move there, and especially if there was work to be had. The glamour of Hollywood also would continue to make people want to move to that vicinity. Even when some people just come to visit, they end up wanting to move to an area nearby. It is getting quite crowded."

"People are fascinated with the fruit orchards. Most people want to pick an orange right off the tree, but so many people were doing just that that they passed a law with a big fine if anyone is caught doing so. If too many persons picked the fruit it would not take very long for the tree to be picked clean and there went the owner's crop and ultimately also his income disappeared along with the crop."

"Some day, we will probably visit down in that area," they all predicted.

"We can hope that nothing like an earthquake, either big or small, ever happens here in this area of the country, although I have read that an earthquake can happen anywhere in the world," they agreed in unison.

"We can all hope that Jennifer locates her grandmother, and that she is all right when she does. A worry like that is not fun. If Jennifer comes to the wedding, we shall ask her."

Chapter 20

❖

"Oh Rosalyn, I just thought of something. You remember when Frank had to chase those cattlemen off his property? Has anything more happened since then? They never tried to take revenge did they?" Martha asked Rosalyn.

"As far as I know, everything has gone smoothly since that time. There have been a few incidents at the site where the house is being built. A few things have disappeared, but the workers have learned to put their tools away and not leave them out. We have found a few cigarette butts around and we are a little bit afraid of the possibility of fire. There is always a chance that a forest fire could happen too and we might lose everything.

There is still quite a bit to do yet" Rosalyn told them. "Also, Frank says most cattlemen are afraid of forest fires so they would be careful of cigarettes possibly starting a fire, which could burn everything in its way. He really feels these people can be caught and maybe so very soon as the sheriff is watching out for them. He doesn't like thieves in his jurisdiction so they had better watch out."

"Thankfully we seem to be having better times so there are fewer people looking for a place to stay, so we haven't had the problem of someone trying to move into the house even though it is not finished." explained Rosalyn.

"People with empty houses will sometimes let someone move in for free just to take care of the place so it does not deteriorate. Most people find that when they let someone move into their empty house, that they will keep it up and when and if they get work, they usually cooperate and will pay their way when they are able to do so. Of course they have to be a little bit careful about who they do let move in, but it always depends on the people themselves. There is not much chance of renting a house the way the economy is so it is better to let a good family move in who will take care of it. Even though the rent is only five dollars a month for a small house, a lot of people don't have even that much money."

"The time may come when you will not want to let someone move into your house because they don't take care of it. A very few people have regretted letting someone move in because they did not appreciate the kindness of the owner and they ended up badly vandalizing the house. It sure is too bad. Times seem to be changing and although times are still very hard they are better than they were a few months back." Rosalyn told the others. "People are not as nice as they used to be"

Martha added "I am glad those cattlemen did not turn around and cause damage. They really did not have any reason to, but who knows nowadays what some people will do when they don't get their own way. We did not have any trouble with them either. I figure they realized their cattle were causing a mess at our place for the children. They did come back and apologize to us, which I did not expect. The one who came back was not the same one who was in charge of the cattle that day they came through. I think the one who came back was the owner and he did not want any trouble."

"Our place is not very far from the national forest and I think that cattleman has directed his foreman or whoever was in charge that they should keep his cattle off of private property. I believe the man wants to keep peace and get along with his neighbors, a far cry from the way that man acted who was here before."

"You know, the price of cattle is not very much at this time. I know you can now buy a steer for thirty-two dollars. Nothing brings much any more. The whole process of earning a living is quite hard with prices the way they are, yet the one buying the goods has a hard time to earn enough to buy even that much."

"I know, thirty-two dollars is a whole months wages, if a person even has a job."

"Oh Martha, did you notice when you were at our place the last time that our small pasture has become a lake?" spoke Jean.

"Oh yes, I sure did." answered Martha. "What in the world happened?"

Jean laughed and informed her "Beavers, lots of Beavers. They decided that the creek would make them a good home, so they have built several dams."

"Won't that ruin some of your pasture land?" exclaimed Martha.

"Oh yes it would, it floods the area," answered Jean.

"What can be done about it"? Martha and Rosalyn asked at almost the same time.

Jean informed them, "According to John, the county extension officers will destroy some of the dams. They will leave a few animals and dams in places where it will do lots of good. They will move those animals from the dams that they destroy, and move them to another location, so they will not destroy the animals themselves. Those beavers can do an immense lot of good if they are located in the right places. Beavers are tremendous dam builders. Their dams are not very easy to destroy. Usually they are blown up after the animals are removed and placed in a better spot."

Rosalyn spoke up, "I hope they will place some on Franks property. There is a very small stream about ½ a mile from the new house location and I think it would make a nice improvement there. I wonder if that can be done?"

"I'll ask John if he will speak to the extension agents when he sees them and they will probably work something out if it is possible. John says the agents were very nice and cooperative with him. They had a hard time destroying the dams those Beavers had built. It seems that Beavers are excellent engineers and really build a strong dam that is very hard to destroy."

Chapter 21

❖

"ROSALYN ARE YOU taking the children to the movies next Saturday?" asked Martha.

"Sure am," replied Rosalyn. "The kids want to see the next chapter of the Gene Autry serial. The feature of the next full movie is with Tex Ritter. We all really enjoy hearing his baritone voice and the kids are delighted when he sings the Boll Weavil Song."

"I think they enjoy the one by Smiley Burnette about the Froggy who went a courting. I even got an autograph from Smiley Burnette for them one time." added Rosalyn.

"I enjoy all the singing too. Just the kid in me, I guess"

"Since my classmate and Geraldine's mother will be here in two weeks, the kids will probably miss that chapter of the Gene Autry serial, unless her mother would like to came along too." further offered Rosalyn.

Jean spoke up "You know, I'll bet her mother might enjoy going with you that day. Why don't you offer to take her along."

"Oh, I will, I will" responded Rosalyn. "I think it might be just the thing to do."

"Say, Jean, I have been wondering if you have heard from Patricia lately? Do you really think her mother is wanting the girls to get married? I sure hope they are careful in picking out a mate. You just cannot be any too careful nowdays."

Jean had received another letter from Patricia who had graduated from school and was now renting an apartment with her sister. She wrote what they were paying for food. Jean was sharing this letter with Martha one day.

Patricia wrote:

July 3, 1934 Dear Jean: After high school my cousin, Artha, married Johnny Burns (you remember Johnny don't you?), and Donna and I went to Fort James to work.

We both got jobs at Grayson's Drive-in on Northwest Turner St. We make the big pay of twenty-five cents an hour. This gives us $2.00 for an 8 hour shift, and we begin at 5 pm and then finish at 2 am with the job of cleaning up afterward. Of course cleaning up is part of having the job. With jobs so scarce, we are glad to have the work no matter what we have to do for it.

We are sharing expenses and since you asked us what it was costing us to live in the city, here is what our food is costing us. We spent the following during the month:

April 1st	1 lb. butter, 1 head lettuce, 1 lb. liver, 2 grapefruit	.67
	2 lb. apples, 2 lb. oranges	.25
2nd	1 qt. milk 3 lb. bananas	.25
3rd	1 qt. milk, 1 loaf bread, 1 pint mayonnaise, small can olives`	.38
8th	1 lb carrots, 1 stalk celery, l loaf bread, l can tomato juice, 1 lb. apples, 1 light globe	.85
	2 lb. cheese	.25
13th	2 qt. milk, ½ doz. Eggs	.32
	1 loaf bread, 1stalk celery, 1 chunk of ice	.50
14th	1 lb. meat, 1 loaf bread	.32
	3 lb. bananas	.15
15th	1 loaf bread, 1 cake, l can hominy, l pkg. Jello, l can sardines	.50
17th	1 qt. milk, 2 lb. oranges, 2 lb. tomatoes, l pie, 2 lb. bacon	.75
20th	1 lb. hamburger, 1 lb. butter, 1 bar soap	.44
22nd	1 loaf bread, 1 pie, l chunk ice	.50
23rd	1 loaf bread, 1 head lettuce, l can tuna fish, 1 qt. ice cream	.45
24th	1 loaf bread, 1 pie,1doz. Rolls, Jello, pudding, 1 qt. milk	.53
26th	1 loaf bread, cookies, 1 pie	.45
27th	1 lb. spaghetti, 2 lb. fruit, 1 lb. hamburger, 1 head lettuce	.40
29th	l pie, 1 cake, 1 lb. hamburger, 1 pudding, 1 can hash, 1 qt milk, 1 lb. butter	<u>1.03</u>
This is what we spent for the month of April		$ 8.99

Can you believe it? One dollar is earned for four hours of work. Each dollar we paid was for one-half of a day's wages. We have to pay five cents for our hamburgers and once in a while we can splurge and pay ten cents for a milk shake. Maybe some day we can afford more. We sure hope prices do not go any higher or else we hope to get better jobs some time. What we spent for groceries amounted to 41/2 days of wages, besides the food we pay for our utilities and the rent is $10.00 a month. We could get a smaller apartment for $2 a month less, but decided we wanted two bedrooms, so we splurged. I hope we can make ends meet. Also, we are real close to work and this way we don't have to pay for bus fare, which keeps some of our costs down. We hope to save by sharing the cost of everything. We know we would have to move back with the folks if either one of us lost out jobs.

Some day we would like to come and visit with you. It sure sounds like you are doing all right. It must be nice that you can raise your own food.

Give my love to Martha and her family.

As ever, Patricia

PS. Some smart-alec kids still come in and ask for a "pine float", but the manager is now charging them 10 cents when they do and we give them a toothpick in a glass of water. I guess they will never learn. Most of them think it is funny and laugh and giggle until they get the bill and have to pay it. Guess that will teach them. The same ones do not come in and try it a second time.

Patricia

"Well, maybe Patricia and her sister will be able to come visit us some day. I do believe they would enjoy spending time in this farming area, don't you? Only I hope they don't come expecting to find a husband. I gathered that their mother may have that in mind for the girls. She wants them to get married. There are a lot of single young men in this area, so it could happen. I won't encourage it though."

"Speaking of prices we only get $32.00 for our steers now when we put them on the market. Hardly worth raising them." volunteered Jean. "What are your apples bringing when you sell them from your orchard?"

"The market for apples now is $1.25 for a 40# box. We have to pay 15 cents a box for picking the fruit. We can hardly break even at this time. We only hope that things will get better before long." answered Martha.

"We are fortunate we don't have to buy water for our orchard. Having our own water supply sure is a lifesaver for our finances. Some of our neighbors have to pay for irrigation and raising money in these hard times can almost sink them financially."

Jean volunteered, "Martha, it surely was a streak of good fortune that you and Bob bought this place when you did."

"Yes, Mother, I sure agree."

"We will have Rosalyn's visitor from back East arriving before long. I believe I am looking forward to their visit as much as Rosalyn is." volunteered Jean.

"I believe I am excited about it too," added Martha." I cannot believe what the lady's thinking is though about Indians and cowboys."

Jean volunteered,"They will be staying at our house while they are here. We will meet them at the stage depot. They are transferring from the train to a bus. I can just see her friend's mother's reaction when we take them around. It seems strange she would have such odd ideas about the western part of the country, but I suppose she has never been in the western part of the United States and must base her ideas on what she sees in the movies. So many people really do not realize that movies are only stories made up of some person's imagination. Even the addition of sound to the movies haven't made a difference to some people."

"It is a little hard to understand how little people know about the history of the western part of the United States." expressed Martha.

"She will certainly know better by the time she goes home. I sure hope she is not offended by the way we show her about this part of the country. We won't make fun of her. She will catch on I am sure. I hope she enjoys this trip for Rosalyn's sake."

"I only wish Rosalyn's friend could stay for the wedding. It is nice though that she can come at all. I'm also glad the woman is bringing her mother."

Martha inquired of Jean if anything had been done for the roads around Mica Peak since winter. The roads were frozen last winter and most have buckled quite badly since they thawed out. If the roads are rough though it will just give the ride around Mica Peak more authenticity for being "western country."

"Rosalyn's friend and her mother should enjoy the scenery around the loop road through the Mica Peak area. That is such a beautiful area with farms, orchards, and truck gardens throughout. I hope we get to see some wild horses and wild burros at that time. They should be down from the hills and feeding close to the road. The day they arrive might be our only chance to make that excursion while they are here. We will be so busy with wedding arrangements that time may be scarce to do much extra then. It will take extra time traveling with the buckboard and horses instead of using an automobile for that trip, but I really want to use the horses then. The rest of the time they are here is pretty well spoken for I'm afraid."

Martha brought up that they were all planning on attending the big annual rodeo event during that time also. Exciting times were ahead for everyone.

Chapter 22

Among all the excitement of the visitors and the wedding plans a letter arrived for Bob from a law firm in Chicago. Because everyone was so busy, no one paid any attention to the letter, and it was put aside without being opened. Probably just some advertising of no importance. It could be opened later on and so it ended up being pushed under all the other clutter of the moment. Right now everyone was very busy. Anyway it sure did not look very important or interesting enough to open up right away. It could wait until a more convenient time. Jean and Rosalyn met Geraldine and her mother, Joy, who insisted they call her by her first name, not Mrs. Foster. Why be formal. She was evidently quite friendly. The ladies felt an immediate like for her and knew the visit would be pleasant, although they wondered if their playing a little trick on them would make them offended at them. It would not take long to tell.

Jean headed out from the stage depot toward Mica Peak. When Jean asked Joy if she was too tired from her trip to spend time sightseeing both Joy and Geraldine quickly exclaimed they were fine. They had slept well on the train and the ride on the bus was not a long one. Besides, they were anxious to see everything they could while they were here in the "Far West." They were not disappointed the first day. The ride around Mica Peak was eventful. They got to see vast farms of growing grain fields, and timber farms where the deer accommodated them by showing up to gaze back at the spectators and the wild mustangs and burros also cooperated beyond their best hopes by showing up. Of course, the animals were curious about the people also. The oohs and ahs were plentiful.

They stopped for a short while to watch at the sawmill where they were busy loading logs and sawing the timber into lumber. All this was new to the visitors. Before they got back to the area where Jean lived they also saw huge dairy farms and large truck gardens. All together it was a vast education for the city lady. Joy did enquire about Indians and cowboys. They told her she would have to wait to see them, probably it would be at the rodeo.

By this time, Jean and Rosalyn figured Geraldine and Joy would most likely be tired and want to rest. They did say they were beginning to tire out but really enjoying everything so far, and Jean headed for her place then. She told the ladies that from then on all sight-seeing would be by automobile.

Joy had caught on by that time that the trip by

buckboard had been a special arrangement for their benefit, and thanked Jean and Rosalyn for the special done just for them. It was a trip they would never forget. The rest of their stay would be different some way and they were looking forward to whatever was provided, and thanked them profusely for taking the time to show them around when they were so busy with everything to do with Rosalyn's wedding and reception. They wished it was possible to stay for the wedding, but glad they were able to come at this time. Now they would enjoy seeing the country homes where their families lived. What a wonderful time they would have if this day was an example of what was ahead of them in the next couple of weeks.

As it turned out Joy was talented with arrangements for weddings and receptions so when she found out the wedding would be in a couple of weeks, she insisted she would do everything she could to help out with anything that could be done so far ahead of time.

Rosalyn, Jean and Martha were happy to hear about her talents and would be very glad for any suggestions and help she could give them. They now all had a goal. Just before they left to go home, Geraldine and Joy would teach them how to do some flower arrangements. It was too bad they had to go home again just a few days before the wedding. There was nothing they could do about it though. Geraldine had to go back to her job. Jobs were too scarce to take a chance on not returning in time.

These friends also brought up different topics regarding marriage and problems that sometimes occur and asked Martha how she handled them. They all knew Martha had not known Bob before their marriage and they were curious because they all noticed that Martha and Bob seemed to get along so well. Martha volunteered that they were not perfect, but they worked at being agreeable with each other. "For one thing, we talk to each other. If we have different opinions about something, we discuss why we think the way we do. Above all, we do not lose our tempers and lash out. That never accomplishes anything. We have a cooling off time if our opinions are really different and then we can discuss why we think the way we do and come to a compromise. Above all, we love each other and work on our problems. You all know how we handled our differing opinion of what to do when we discovered the money Jackson had hidden in the trunk after selling the farm I had inherited. Bob did not feel it was his to spend so he asked me put it away for the future and I had wanted to use it to buy this home we now have. I used some of it to fix up the house the way I wanted it, and we took a third of it and invested in livestock. I paid for the livestock out of the money, and he did the work involved with the animals. This worked out for the benefit of our whole family. We had come to this agreement the next morning after finding the money. We had both thought over night of what to do about it, and the arrangement has worked out for both of us."

"Bob makes me feel like an important person. He does not criticize me when I make a mistake, and I do make mistakes at times. He is tender and caring and always jovial as you have undoubtedly noticed. I can fully trust him. We try to understand each other, which I think is very important in any relationship. We do not yell at each other and try to never under any circumstances to hurt our partner's feelings. Hurting feelings leaves scars and scars leave nasty marks. Consideration for our partner is a priority with us and it reflects right down to the children also."

"You know, the Bible has some very good advice too. Proverbs 24 verses 3 and 4 says "By wisdom a household will be built up, and by discernment it will prove firmly established. And by knowledge will the interior rooms be filled with all precious and pleasant things of value." "The precious things fill a happy household with such qualities as love, loyalty, godly fear, and faith. A person with discernment is able to understand the thoughts and feelings of his or her mate. We try to use consideration and kindness in all our dealings with each other and with other people. It works for us."

"How clever you both handled it," they all agreed. Then Rosalyn wanted to know what she did when the kids used bad words, which all kids were inclined to try. Martha smiled and said sweetly, "I sit them in a corner and make them repeat the word over and over and over. By the time I let them quit saying the word, they never want to say or hear it again ever. After saying the word about a dozen times they thoroughly hate the word. It seems to work real well."

"I'll have to remember that if I ever need that with my children in the future," Rosalyn spoke up.

While they were visiting, the subject of the state of the economy came into their conversation. The depression conditions was on everyone's mind. Those who had jobs were the lucky ones. Geraldine and Joy were glad that Martha and Jean were getting by so well, even if they didn't have a lot of luxuries. Of course the subject of Don and Annabelle and their family and his business also came up. They were wondering how things were going with Don's family. Joy remarked how beautifully little Mary was dressed and also Don and the boys wore such beautiful suits, which showed that Don must be doing extremely well with his business in order to afford such expensive clothes for himself and for the children.

Jean and Martha caught onto what she was getting at and both laughed and asked Joy if she would like to know how they could afford to dress the family in such beautiful clothes. "Don married a very industrious woman who was quite clever with ideas and her sewing machine. She goes to thrift stores, finds used dresses with nice material and of a size to furnish material enough to make something out of it. She gets expensive material at a reasonable price that way. By cutting and altering those dresses she makes those lovely dresses for Mary. She does the same for suits for the boys also."

Joy and Geraldine gasped, "Oh, what a clever idea. That is wonderful. I would never have thought of such a thing."

"Yes, she dresses the family in stylish clothes at a very small cost. I kind of wondered about it myself until one day I saw her shopping at the local thrift store and then I knew. She will sew for my girls too if I furnish the material. This helps all of us."

"I sew a little bit, but I do not have the talent that Annabelle has." offered Jean.

Martha also added, "I think she also buys and alters suits for Don. I know the thrift stores do get in some expensive suits for men sometimes and Don always looks neat and well dressed, really too well dressed for what he makes at his business to afford expensive suits. It is all possible because Annabelle is so clever with her sewing machine. I am glad for him."

"Life is a financial struggle for everyone and we all hope this depression will end soon. We only hope we don't get dragged into that war that is going on over in Europe. It sure does not look very good. I am afraid if we get into that war Don's oldest boy might be caught into it. He is getting to that age now. I don't want to see us in any war. I remember a bit of what happened from 1914 through 1918 and I don't like it at all. It worries me."

"Yes, honey, it worries all of us, but if we were attacked like some of those European countries were, we would probably be in it over night without fail. War is horrible, no matter how you look at it or where it is fought."

Jean turned to the others and said, "let's change the subject to something a bit more pleasant, like this wedding that is coming up in a few days and how you enjoyed your visit to our western part of the country. I know times are unsettled but right now I really do not want to think of unpleasant things like wars and unemployment and the sadness that goes with all that.

They all agreed. Joy spoke up and assured Rosalyn and her friends that she was glad she had been straightened up about the cowboys and Indians. "I don't know why I didn't figure out that what I had seen in the movies was only a figment of someone's imagination. It sure was imagination in my mind and I feel a bit foolish about it. I guess I am like a lot of people who do not stop and think. Also I know I do not have any real knowledge of the history of our country. I will know better in the future and certainly I will go to the library and learn about the early pioneers of our land and what really went on throughout the years. I will also try to learn more of the current events going on now. I and several of my friends need to get our heads out of the sand and learn about people who live someplace besides in New York City and quit basing my opinions on movies."

Joy continued, "At least I did not have the idea that the mail was still carried by Pony Express. That idea would have really been too much. I did learn though that your mail comes by the carrier using a horse and buggy in the winter time. I guess he has found that it is easier to get through the deep snow and muddy ruts that way. I also noticed that while we are here, this being summer time, he is coming by automobile. Someone also told me that this carrier delivers mail to your neighbors without taking the letters back to the post office. He just cancels the stamp and leaves the letter in their mailbox. I like that idea. You can get word to your friends and neighbors really fast that way. It's wonderful, the help the carrier gives by delivering groceries and even passengers. You have it made."

"Yes, it is very handy to be on a rural carrier route. That is why it is called a RFD route as part of our address. Like you said, the carrier can cancel the stamp without taking the letter back to the post office, but it is only if the letter goes to someone on his route between our house and the post office. It works out that way and it surely is nice."

Joy laughed and commented about how she was enjoying all the scenery she had been shown while here, and the experiences encountered. I even enjoyed seeing the animal that looked so much like a funny kind of horse. That one I said looked like a horse with long legs but still wasn't a horse. You called it a moose. I still think its head looked like a horse to me even if the rest of it didn't. The baby moose was so very cute though. Made me want to pet it. Don't laugh at my ignorance. I am quickly learning. I guess I have lived in the city too long without paying attention to other parts of the world. That will change from now on. Thanks to you.

"My grandmother told me about some of her early experiences one time when I was a little girl. She and Grandpa lived in the North Dakota territory and she would clean birds for the hunters in the fall. She said she was not afraid of the Indians as she had made friends with them when she first came there. She also told me about carrying something she called an Arkansas toothpick. When I asked her what that was she said it was a double edged, razor sharp knife with a point like a needle. She also told me it was not to protect her from the Indians, but the riff-raff who were dangerous ruffians who sometimes traveled around the country and preyed on women who happened to be alone when their men folks had to be away for one reason or another." volunteered Geraldine.

Martha and Jean both remarked, "I guess we all have to be careful, whether it is this generation or one earlier, or in the future I suppose there will always be those we have to be aware of."

Geraldine confided, "We have both learned a lot and I am sure my mother has enjoyed this visit with all of you as much as I have. While I did not have those ideas my mother had about Indians attacking you folks and cowboys carrying guns and shooting people on the street, I did learn how hard you all worked to keep food on the table for us as well as for yourselves. I have really and truly enjoyed this visit. Some day I want to come again."

"Good girl. We want you to come again, both of you." everyone spoke up agreeably. Geraldine then spoke up again that she noticed how well Martha and Bob got along. "You both seem so happy and it is obvious that you get along really well. So many couples seem to fight and a large number of couples seem to head for the divorce court within a short time after they are married. I know you and Bob did not know each other a long time before you married."

Martha then told them, "Yes, we really were total strangers when we met and got married. I do not recommend this to anyone. We were both very fortunate that our personalities were compatible as well as our determination to make things work out."

"You never seem to get mad at each other. I notice you both seem so calm all the time." brought out Rosalyn. "How do you do it? Could we talk about it some more. I sure want some lessons for my forthcoming marriage."

"We try to be thoughtful towards each other. We talk things over without losing our tempers and never, never say anything to deliberately hurt each others feelings. Oh, we do not agree on everything but by discussing our differences we come to a solution. We have also learned how to please each other. It all takes work and we never carry a grudge. A grudge never accomplishes anything. We also never argue in front of other people, which is embarrassing to everyone else as well as ourselves. Above all, we also try to be good to each other. If I disagree with Bob or he disagrees with me, we talk it over without losing our tempers. We never forget that we love each other."

"This is a good lesson for all of us," Rosalyn and Geraldine both chorused. "So many people argue about money and the way it is spent. How do you handle that?" they asked.

"We keep each other informed about our income and what we can afford to spend.

I try to be careful about what I buy. Because I am careful, Bob knows he does not have to worry. He never scolds me about what I spend, but because I am careful with our funds, he must feel relaxed about the way I handle it. Sometimes he tells me I am too careful, but I know he works too hard for me to waste either money or materials. When the banks failed, we lost most of what we had deposited, but fortunately we have been able to survive with what we have without being in poverty. While not affluent, we have it quite comfortable in comparison to most people at this time. Living on a farm we are able to raise our food and have our own meat. We do not suffer as some have."

"I will keep all of this in mind, Martha, and I really thank you for the lesson. I hope I can remember all of this and use the information to help make my marriage to Frank a happy one."

Everyone kept on talking about the happy event of the marriage of Frank and Rosalyn that would be going on in a few days. Then, Jean gave Joy a pretty doily she had made and that Joy had admired. Joy made the remark that she was going to keep it for special occasions.

Geraldine laughed at her mother and remarked, "Mother, I had some friends who went on a special trip to New York a few years back. While there, her husband had bought her a very nice pretty scarf. When they got home,

Beth put it in a dresser drawer to keep for some "special occasion." She died about 9 years later, and her husband was gathering up some items to take to the funeral parlor. When he came across this prettily wrapped package, still wrapped up, he opened it up, then placed the contents with the clothes going to the funeral home. It was the scarf, which she had never used. It was too bad, but the special occasion turned out to be her funeral, and nine years were wasted."

Geraldine went on "I never save anything for special occasions since that time as they never come. Use it every day as every day in your life is a special occasion. Don't delay or keep anything that can bring joy into your life as waiting for a special occasion may only be your funeral."

Joy assured everyone she was going to use the doily every single day as a special occasion and it would remind her of Jean and this wonderful trip, which of itself was a very special occasion.

They all agreed that none of them would ever again keep "things" for special occasions. It was a lesson learned for all of them.

Chapter 23

The Reception And
The Forgotten Letter

GERALDINE AND JOY went home and the guests for the wedding started arriving a few days later. Making arrangements with nearby motels became a time consuming job.

It would have been nice to put them up in their homes, but Jean and Martha found out there would be too many for them to handle. Those who arrived by automobile could be sent to the hotels that were a little farther away. Some of the guests would be coming for quite a distance. Of course Frank was looking forward to seeing his friends and relatives from California. Because of the distance, not too many of Rosalyn's friends would come, but there would be a couple of cousins. Jean thought maybe Patricia and her sister would come also. They had not said they could definitely come, although they wanted to. The two girls had been invited but did not know if their financial situation would make it possible to afford coming. They were surely going to come if they could arrange it in any way at all. Even Uncle Curtis might be able to come. He sure wanted to according to what he had written. He was going to try very hard to make it. He wanted to see the family that he missed. Their living so far away kept them apart too long.

The letter from some law firm in Chicago was still laying unopened on Bob's desk. It ended up underneath other items that were not important. In fact they did not even think of it with all the excitement of the wedding going on. They did not attach it to anything important anyway. That letter had to wait for its turn for attention. After all they did not know anyone in Chicago, least of all some law firm probably just advertising something to sell. They would open it when they had time if they ever remembered it.

Some people started arriving the week before the wedding date. A few were even coming by air plane. Things were sure getting modern. It was hard to imagine anyone getting there in an air ship. They had planned on sightseeing around the area. Fortunately they were not expecting Jean or Martha to entertain them, knowing they would be busy with everything to do with the wedding plans. Actually, this occasion was looked forward to by the whole community. It was always nice to have visitors from other areas and sometimes this is the way to make friends all over the country. Life was more interesting when you could get to talk to people from other parts of the country. Exchanging experiences with someone else was always the way to make new friends and it kept your attention. Besides you could have a place to visit when or if you went to where the other person lived.

Of course Frank's relatives started arriving from California. They wanted to meet the bride before the ceremony because they thought there would not be much chance to get acquainted afterward.

Even with all the excitement of the arriving guests all the final wedding arrangements were completed without further interruption. Everyone was excited about how nice everything went, The lovely place for the reception and several people spoke of how they were so impressed with this area they thought they wanted to buy a place like this for themselves. They really did not realize how hard Bob and Martha had worked to make everything work out for both themselves and for Rosalyn and Frank.

The reception was nearly over when little Bobby came running to Martha with a message for Martha and his father. He was really excited because the mailman wanted to see them because they had to sign for a letter he had for them. Bob excused himself and went to the house to see what was so important that the mail carrier had to deliver a registered letter on this day of all times.

When Bob examined the envelope he recognized it as from the law firm they had received the letter from a couple of weeks before and had never opened. In fact he had actually forgotten about the former letter and it had been buried under some other items left on his desk that he had thought unimportant. Upon opening the letter, he became a bit too excited, but did not want to upset anyone else on this happy day and decided to wait until later to show the letter to Martha. No use ruining this special occasion for anyone. He had to put up a good front for the rest of the day even though he was worried about its contents and how it would affect their future. He thought the past was dead and this was something to remind them it was not dead yet.

All went well for the wedding ceremony. The beauty of the surroundings of the farm setting that Bob and Martha had fixed up, not only for the wedding, but for their family had everyone expressing their admiration. Many spoke up to say they thought it would be a good idea if they could also move to this area to live. Everything was so nice.

All the people they met were also very friendly. The guests from out of town were cordially invited to visit the local guests. Many new friends were made and promises of further friendships were discussed between many of the guests.

The wedding and reception over, Frank and Rosalyn sneaked off to go on their honeymoon. Of course they must have had help from someone, but everyone was having so much fun they did not notice the couple was gone until it was too late. Their secret destination had been kept by their good friends, Bob and Martha. The party kept on for a couple more hours before everyone left after the guests expressed to the hosts that they had really enjoyed everything.

Chapter 24

※

The Letter Opened

A$_{FTER}$ $_{EVERYONE}$ $_{WAS}$ gone, Bob showed the letter to Martha, even though he had really not wanted to. He was afraid she would be upset with the information. He knew it might bring back those old memories of Jackson and the loss of her infant daughter and he loved her too much to want her to have such pain again. But, there was nothing he could do since the letter concerned both of them.

Martha read the letter, and in handing it back to Bob, remarked, "We will just have to see what we can do with it and take care of whatever happens."

The letter contained information that they had inherited some property that once belonged to some of Jackson's ancestors and had never been probated until now… It was located somewhere near their farm in Mesa Ridge and also concerned Bob as he was also a descendant of one of those ancestors. How could that be. It was going to take a while to sort out all the people involved, but it did appear to come down mostly to the two of them. Seems like everyone else was deceased.

Where in the world was this property located? It was reported to be near Mesa Ridge, but they did not know of any property near them that it could be, unless it was that old forgotten Norland place between their old home and this one here. There had not been anyone there for over thirty or forty years. The family had started to dig a mine and had evidently found a vein of silver in it, but due to circumstances had never followed up on it. The young folks had moved away when the parents passed away. The younger children wanted to have nothing to do with the property and just left it as it was. None of them must have left any heirs other than those that came on down to Bob and Martha. They would have to find out the connection later. It was evidently necessary to contact the law firm to get any further information about it.

How come they were both involved? As far as Bob and Martha were concerned, they were not related to the old folks in any way that they knew of. Of course it had to be that Jackson and Bob may have been related in some distant way. Sure was an odd situation, especially if that was so. Jackson must have known about the property though. Maybe he was heading for Mesa Ridge when he sold Martha's farm. He did seem to have something in mind even though he would not tell Martha anything about his plans.

There was nothing left to do except contact that Chicago law firm to see what this was all about. That was something they could do by calling them on the telephone first of all. It was a surprising development that was very unexpected.

What they were told was that Jackson had inherited a portion of the property from an aunt who had been married to one of the original owners. The lawyer had tried to trace down all of the ones involved and it had been quite a job as so many of the original heirs had died and many of the survivors had married or remarried and tracing them down had been quite a big job. Now it seemed that the only thing left was to trace down the heirs of one Jackson Johnson and they had heard that Mr. Johnson had married but that his wife and child had been killed in a landslide several years ago. What he needed to find out is if there were any other heirs before Robert Mason could inherit his share of the property. It did seem that Robert Mason was clearly the last survivor of one of the original owners of this property. He wanted to know if Robert Mason knew of any other heirs that one Jackson Johnson may have had. The Chicago lawyer was surprised to find out that the wife of Jackson Johnson had erroneously been reported as killed, and that she was still living and was now married to Robert Mason. Since Martha had been married to Jackson Johnson she was the heir they were seeking. This left the property to Martha and Bob to do whatever they wanted to do with the property as soon as proof of who they were was submitted. All the papers would be signed and the property would be turned over to them.

It turned out that because Martha had been married to Jackson that was what had made her his heir. Bob was very distantly related to one of the heirs to the property, probably through his great grandmother on his mothers side of the family, also evidently through marriages and inheritances after the deaths of other heirs. It appeared to be a complicated affair.

Martha then began to realize that this property is probably what Jackson was headed for when he sold Martha's farm. All this was now making a bit of sense to what had happened in the past. Now what!!! They also found out the property was the old Norland claim. This was property they were already familiar with.

Martha's uncle Curtis Verne Andrews had come to the wedding of Rosalyn and Frank and later when he heard about this new development of the inheritance of the property he told them he was interested if they wanted to sell that property. He had been greatly impressed with this country since he had arrived and since his sister and niece already lived in the area he would love to find something for himself. He had actually been inquiring around about property and something nearby would work out really well for him.

It was then that Bob and Martha remembered the earlier remark Martha had made about her uncle Curtis being one who would love to restore that old Norland property. He was young and willing to work to fix something up if he liked it. When they described the property to Curtis, he wanted to look it over. The fact it was back in the hills a ways did not deter him at all. He asked them if there was a road to the place and if it was nothing more than a trail, maybe he could build a road or fix one up. They would go look the property over the next day. Of course they would have to wait until all the paper work was complete for transferring the property over to them before they could sell the property, but in the meantime he could decide if he wanted the property.

By the time all of this had transpired Frank and Rosalyn were back from their honeymoon so Martha asked Rosalyn to stay with the children while she and Bob and Uncle Curtis went to look over the Norland property. When he saw the property and looked it over, he said he was positive it was something he would like to try to take over and make it into a very livable place. By putting a roof on the cabin it could be lived in at least until a bigger house could be built, although it was big enough for a bachelor to live in as it was. By pruning the orchard the trees could probably be reclaimed, and there was certainly enough land that could be farmed if the trees were cleared out. He could use the trees for lumber to build whatever he would need for buildings. Bob told him there was a sawmill in the region that would probably saw the logs for him if he supplied the trees and they could do the work in exchange for some trees for themselves. It was then that Curtis said he would negotiate with the sawmill to log the timber and also maybe it could be arranged to have the loggers also build the road into the place. Obviously something was in his mind to make things work out for him.

One of the former owners must have been quite industrious as there was a log trough from a spring that had brought water towards the orchard to irrigate the trees. This is probably what had kept the trees alive all those years and while they needed to be pruned they seemed to be in pretty fair condition. They sampled some of the fruit and it was good. Uncle Curtis said he would look into the mine but he did not think he would pursue that part of the property, at least at this time. Yes, he was very interested in this piece of property. He could see all kinds of possibilities for it, and he was young enough to be able to make something out of this kind of property. When Bob and Martha teased him about his maybe having a wife in mind, he seriously told them that maybe he just might have someone in mind. They did not pursue that subject any further and headed back to their house. Now they felt a bit better about pursuing this inheritance further.

Both Bob and Martha were happy that this inheritance was something that could be disposed of right away as they did not want more property. There was plenty to do with what they already owned. By selling the inheritance they would be able to pay off the rest of the mortgage on their farm. Fortunately Uncle Curtis had been employed during the depression years so was in a financial position to pay cash for this piece of real estate.

The Chicago lawyer had been busy and by the time Uncle Curtis was ready to buy this old place he had the paper work all cleared up and was able to fix up the sale from Bob and Martha to Curtis.

Epilogue

"Who cares who milks the cow" Martha was told
How many women would be so bold
To feed someone else's child at her breast
A hungry baby would be her guest.
Now who does care who milks the cow.
It accomplished wonders we know, somehow.
It fed the babies once, then again it was twice.
Now everyone's happy, isn't that nice.
Bob and Martha in passing this place with such charm
Didn't know that later they would own this old farm.
Their families were joined by marriages it seemed.
That so many years later it would be redeemed.
They would inherit this land unknown to them now.
And solve the mystery of why
someone had to milk the cow.
The Norland family so many there were

Did not farm this land for Douglas Fir.
But silver ore is what they sought
They found a little, but it was for naught.
Old John Norland up and died one day
The silver they found sure did not pay
They tried for gold but it was not to be
The heirs just said "It's not for me."
So they all moved away without a thought
Left it alone just to end up for naught.
Undivided it lay for many a year
Heirs there were some, but title wasn't clear.
Those heirs died slowly without leaving a clue
Until it seemed it left them with only a few.
Finally when someone decided to sell
The job to clear title to a lawyer fell.
He found heir Jackson and learned he had died
Read the obituary and found that it lied.
His heir turned up alive, it was Martha you see.
So now she and Bob owned this old property.
To sell the property is what they wanted to do
So a ready and willing buyer they now had a good clue
It solved the mystery of Martha's sudden move west
That ended up sad, but turned out for the best.
Martha loved Bob dearly, no doubt you can see
Little Bobby gained a mother and Martha became free
Bob gained a good wife to replace one who wasn't a joy.
All are now happy, the husband,
the wife, and the little boy.

Many years later after all the children had grown up, they went through several wars, with sadness and all that followed. There was World War II and the United

States was drawn into that war with the bombing of Pearl Harbor in Hawaii. Viet Nam, Korea followed and all the rest of the many conflicts and Don Fisher's older son, Ray, sad to say, lost his life in one of them. Frank and Rosalyn had finished building their home and were settled quite happily with their two children. Rosalyn had kept her teaching position until the children arrived. The community had loved her as teacher and as a neighbor.

Bob and Martha lived to be in their nineties, had many grandchildren who loved them dearly. The greatest tribute was given by young Bobby. Now all grown up and a father of his own children he claimed Martha was the best Mother of all time. With great love in his heart he had nothing but praise for her. He told the family later that he was proud that he had been the one who was entitled to say "**Who Cares Who Milks The Cow**" because that was what saved his life and the whole family had a right to be very proud of Martha, and the term was an endearing one to him.